BAT
IN THE DINING ROOM

BY **CRESCENT DRAGONWAGON**
ILLUSTRATED BY **S. D. SCHINDLER**

MARSHALL CAVENDISH   **NEW YORK**

Marshall Cavendish, 99 White Plains Road, Tarrytown, New York 10591
The text of this book is set in 14 point Stempel Schneidler
The illustrations are rendered in colored pencil and watercolor on pastel paper
Printed in Italy   First edition   6 5 4 3 2 1

Library of Congress Cataloging-in-Publication Data
Dragonwagon, Crescent. Bat in the dining room / Crescent Dragonwagon ; illustrated by S.D. Schindler.   p.   cm.
Summary: When a bat flies into a hotel restaurant, Melissa comes to the rescue.
ISBN 0-7614-5007-6 (library binding)   [1. Bats—Fiction. 2. Stories in rhyme.] I. Schindler, S. D., ill. II. Title.
PZ8.3.D77Bat 1997   [E]—dc21   96-54894 CIP AC

For Louis and Elsie Freund, who continue to open doors and encourage flight.
Love, C. D.

To Jim, McKey, Philip, Nellie, Winston, and Claire—good sports and bat friendly
S. D. S.

A bat flew into the dining room,
at the hotel restaurant by the lake.
Mistake.

The open window
must have called to it,
called it away
from sail and flit
from bat wings
from bat things
in from outside
from above the lake.
Mistake,
that bat in the hotel dining room.

Perhaps it fell?
No way to tell, or if it flew
down the chimney:
no one knew.
But suddenly, suddenly,
in the warm night air
in the hotel dining room
it was there
just a bat
confused and scared.

For a moment no one noticed it or saw
it circling wildly:
The ceiling high, the fans a-twirl,
the mothers fathers aunts and uncles
boys and girls—
cousins in-laws sisters brothers
Melissa, quiet, with the others
Waiters in their black and whites
summer evening, coming night.
Menus murmurs conversation
ordinary June vacation
"I think I'll start with the … fruit cup."
who would have even thought, "look up"?
Then someone did.

A women in a large green hat
looked up and saw it and screamed "Bat!"
and ducked and screamed again, then more—

"A bat a bat a bat!"—the door
was rushed by panicked families
who crouched and gazed up frightenedly
covering heads with sunburnt arms
as if that bat could do them harm,
the babies bursting into tears
at all the screaming clutching fears
of parents cousins uncles aunts—
like that the dining room was cleared,
the patrons in the lobby.

Well! I never!
Did you ever!
Was it hiding in the curtains?
We're never coming *here* again, that's certain!
Ugh! I hate bats worse than anything—
It could have gotten in my hair!
Tell me, is it still in there?

But all that running for the door
and screaming just confused the bat still more

In vain the maître d' cried, "Please!
don't be alarmed, I have no doubt
in just a moment we'll have it out,
and dinner on the house."

Is there no one anywhere who guesses
how that thing which panicked them might be,
that dark gray bat shape, delicate,
frightened, circling crazily?
And could they ever, even one, think to feel
that bat's bat-fright,
spinning spinning spinning from outside, trapped
inside a strange enclosed and lit-up night?
Not even one in sympathy?
Yes. Melissa.
No one saw her yet.

The waiters and the chef talk loudly
in the kitchen by the dining room.
"Well, look, if I get a ladder, and a broom—"
"If we could stun it, catch it—"
"If we open all the windows wide—"
"Let's think, what else could we try?"

And bat, poor bat, its pitch too high
for anyone to hear, but in its panicked flight,
if anyone had looked and really seen
they could have heard (from just the way it moved),
a terrified cry
and seen its beautiful ridged wings beating like a heart
fluttering like moths . . .
where is it, how can it get out, how
did it get caught?

It wants its home night sky
no horizon chopped by roof and fan
just darkening air above and clear.

The bat careens into a fan blade and is stunned
and plummets to the floor
as conversation raises to a fever pitch
beyond the dining room door.
A boy peeking through the lobby glass, saw it, said
"It fell, it fell, oh good, I think it's dead!"

But Melissa hadn't run, she'd dropped to the floor,
under the table, cloth-draped in white,
watching, listening with all her might.
Strange Melissa, at school they called her weird,
that night she lifted up the tablecloth and peered:
and saw the bat, stunned, flapping on the floor
and she alone thought how the bat might feel.

And so she crept across the carpeted floor
and reached the outside exit door.
The others, panicked, had forgotten it.
Melissa knew, since only just that morning
she had noticed that outside door, exploring,
when she'd gone out herself, walking.

She loved her family, yes, but all that talking:
Mandy, her sister, Charles, her brother,
Mama, Daddy, Fred, the noisy others—
no quiet, not enough sometimes to think a single thought
sometimes Melissa just took off, escaped that feeling caught.

On her morning walk she'd seen that door,
just as she'd noticed, quiet, a thousand things or more.
A cardinal on a telephone wire
that the third swing on the left was higher
a padlocked gate, some lichen on a stone
a high-up bird's nest, which she left alone
the way the frogs got silent by the lake
when she walked close; and that the water
was more gray than blue
a thousand things that I or you
might not notice, might not see,
Melissa saw that morning, including
the dining room's outside exit door.

Was this seeing why Melissa knew that
the one most frightened of it all was the bat?

Her mother, in the lobby, just then missed her.
"Mandy! Where's Melissa, where's your sister!"
And as Melissa crawled out from beneath the table,
the bat began to fly again, since it was able.
"Ah, it's not dead, let's shoot it!" cried the watching boy,
seeing the bat, then added "Hey, there's a girl still there,
look at that, a girl in there, with that bat!"

"Melissa!" screamed her mother
racing for the lobby door,
"If I've told that child once, it's been
a thousand times or more—"
But before she could go in, Melissa reached
that secret door.

The door had a sign lit up in red:
emergency exit only, it said.
Melissa stood and pushed it, stepped outside
and held it open. "Come on, bat!" she cried,
but very softly, no one could hear.
"Come on bat, come on bat, come on out here!"

The bat continued circling in the dining room.
The chef was waiting, with a broom.
The maître d' was calling Department of Wildlife,
the little boy said, "Shoot it! Hit it! Throw a knife!"
But Melissa crouched there in the dark, kept saying
"Come on, bat,"

and with each circle the bat came closer
as if it smelled the soft night air
as if it saw the outside dark
as if it hoped but didn't dare
believe it might find its way again
back out of there
to dream of circling, darkling night
to lift bat-wings to be bat-right
to swoop and glide above the lake
to leave this strange enclosed mistake.

The wildlife officer had a gun
it would not kill but only stun
he drove up in his truck, he parked

but even then the bat moved there—
towards that piece of dark, a square
Melissa's opened door the way
the bat could fly out free, away,
and swoop out into nighttime.

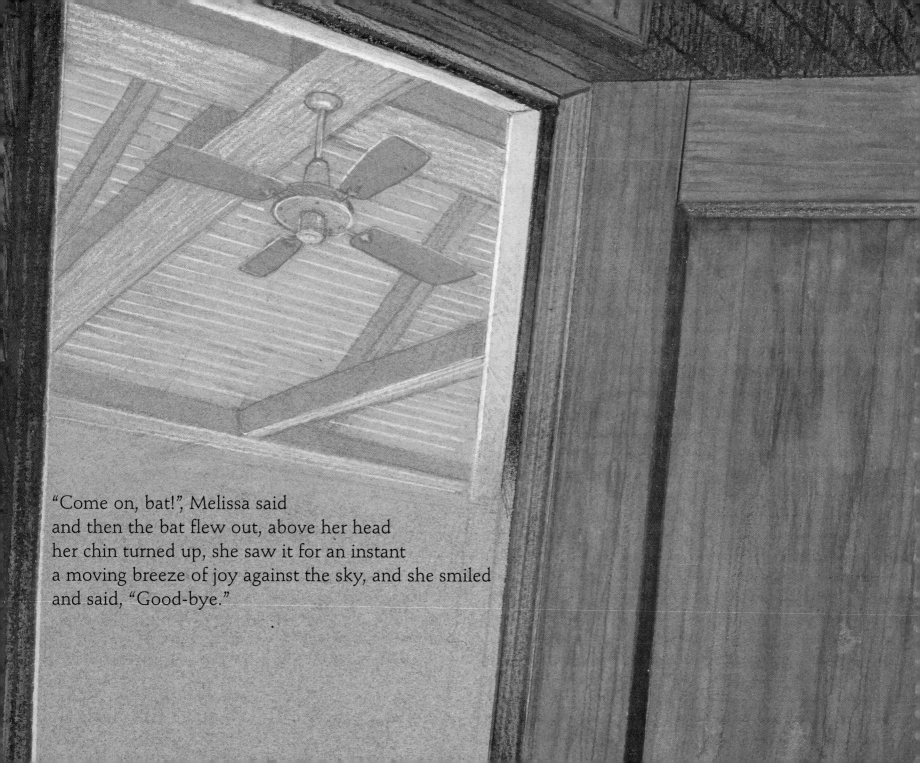

"Come on, bat!", Melissa said
and then the bat flew out, above her head
her chin turned up, she saw it for an instant
a moving breeze of joy against the sky, and she smiled
and said, "Good-bye."

An hour later, all was calm,
dinner served to all guests, free,
and everyone discussed the bat excitedly,
and how brave the little girl'd been.

They fussed over Melissa,
called her kind to animals, and smart:
but no one had a clue
no one even knew
what was in her heart.
She smiled politely and said "Thank you very much,"
And "All I did was open up a door,"
And "I just remembered that exit from before."

But that night, when she crawled into bed
Melissa remembered, smiling in the dark,
the joyful moment when the bat
flew out and free above her head
and thought of it a-swoop a-glide
its panic ended, flit and soar
and that she'd held the open door;
now in its night, bat-circling and bat-limber
and thought, "I hope that bat's forgotten
this night, which I will always remember."

J
E
DRA

Dragonwagon,
Crescent.

Bat in the dining
room.

DATE			

BAKER & TAYLOR

DISEASES & DISORDERS

Bipolar Disorder

Melissa Abramovitz

LUCENT BOOKS
A part of Gale, Cengage Learning

GALE
CENGAGE Learning·

Detroit • New York • San Francisco • New Haven, Conn • Waterville, Maine • London

GALE
CENGAGE Learning·

LIBRARY OF CONGRESS CATALOGING-IN-PUBLICATION DATA

Abramovitz, Melissa, 1954-
  Bipolar disorder / by Melissa Abramovitz.
    p. cm. -- (Diseases and disorders)
  Summary: "This series objectively and thoughtfully explores topics of medical importance. Books include sections on a description of the disease or disorder and how it affects the body, as well as diagnosis and treatment of the condition"-- Provided by publisher.
  Includes bibliographical references and index.
  ISBN 978-1-4205-0853-6 (hardback)
  1. Manic-depressive illness--Juvenile literature. 2. Manic-depressive illness--Treatment--Juvenile literature.
  RC516.A28 2012
  616.89'5--dc23

                                                          2012002942

Lucent Books
27500 Drake Rd.
Farmington Hills, MI 48331

ISBN-13: 978-1-4205-0853-6
ISBN-10: 1-4205-0853-9

Printed in the United States of America
1 2 3 4 5 6 7 16 15 14 13 12

Table of Contents

"The Most Difficult Puzzles Ever Devised"

Charles Best, one of the pioneers in the search for a cure for diabetes, once explained what it is about medical research that intrigued him so. "It's not just the gratification of knowing one is helping people," he confided, "although that probably is a more heroic and selfless motivation. Those feelings may enter in, but truly, what I find best is the feeling of going toe to toe with nature, of trying to solve the most difficult puzzles ever devised. The answers are there somewhere, those keys that will solve the puzzle and make the patient well. But how will those keys be found?"

Since the dawn of civilization, nothing has so puzzled people—and often frightened them, as well—as the onset of illness in a body or mind that had seemed healthy before. A seizure, the inability of a heart to pump, the sudden deterioration of muscle tone in a small child—being unable to reverse such conditions or even to understand why they occur was unspeakably frustrating to healers. Even before there were names for such conditions, even before they were understood at all, each was a reminder of how complex the human body was, and how vulnerable.

While our grappling with understanding diseases has been frustrating at times, it has also provided some of humankind's most heroic accomplishments. Alexander Fleming's accidental discovery in 1928 of a mold that could be turned into penicillin has resulted in the saving of untold millions of lives. The isolation of the enzyme insulin has reversed what was once a death sentence for anyone with diabetes. There have been great strides in combating conditions for which there is not yet a cure, too. Medicines can help AIDS patients live longer, diagnostic tools such as mammography and ultrasounds can help doctors find tumors while they are treatable, and laser surgery techniques have made the most intricate, minute operations routine.

This "toe-to-toe" competition with diseases and disorders is even more remarkable when seen in a historical continuum. An astonishing amount of progress has been made in a very short time. Just two hundred years ago, the existence of germs as a cause of some diseases was unknown. In fact, it was less than 150 years ago that a British surgeon named Joseph Lister had difficulty persuading his fellow doctors that washing their hands before delivering a baby might increase the chances of a healthy delivery (especially if they had just attended to a diseased patient)!

Each book in Lucent's Diseases and Disorders series explores a disease or disorder and the knowledge that has been accumulated (or discarded) by doctors through the years. Each book also examines the tools used for pinpointing a diagnosis, as well as the various means that are used to treat or cure a disease. Finally, new ideas are presented—techniques or medicines that may be on the horizon.

Frustration and disappointment are still part of medicine, for not every disease or condition can be cured or prevented. But the limitations of knowledge are being pushed outward constantly; the "most difficult puzzles ever devised" are finding challengers every day.

Why the Increasing Numbers of Bipolar Disorder?

The prevalence of bipolar disorder (BD) has increased dramatically over the last twenty years, particularly in young people, but experts are not sure why. BD is characterized by extreme mood and behavior swings, from mania to depression and back. It can affect anyone of any age, but the National Institute of Mental Health (NIMH) reports that at least half of all cases begin before age twenty-five.

Over 6 million people in the United States now suffer from BD, and doctors suspect that many more are undiagnosed. A study reported in 2007 found that the number of youth (aged zero to nineteen) diagnosed with the disease increased from 25 per 100,000 in 1994–1995 to 1,003 per 100,000 in 2002–2003—a fortyfold increase. The number of adults almost doubled, increasing from 905 per 100,000 in 1994–1995 to 1,679 per 100,000 in 2002–2003.

Previously Underdiagnosed?

Some experts have proposed that the reason for these dramatic increases is that BD used to be underdiagnosed and is currently overdiagnosed. Mental illnesses in general used to be widely underdiagnosed, in part because they carried an even greater stigma than they do today. Being told that a family member had a mental illness was, and still is, a source of shame for many people. This is because mental illness was regarded as a weakness of character rather than as a real disease with biological causes.

But in recent years, scientists have proved that diseases like BD have a biological basis. This has reduced the stigma somewhat, particularly in Western countries, and people are more willing to seek a diagnosis for a medical illness than for something that simply carries the label "crazy." In less-developed countries, mental illness still carries a tremendous amount of shame, and people are extremely reluctant to admit that they have a mental disorder. Health experts believe this may help explain why a study reported in March 2011 found that the United States has the highest prevalence of BD (4.4 percent of the population) among eleven countries surveyed. India has the lowest (1.1 percent).

Another factor that led to widespread underdiagnosis of BD in the United States was that many patients were misdiagnosed with other disorders. A study reported in 1999 in the *Journal of Affective Disorders* found that doctors did not diagnose BD in 40 percent of the people who should have received this diagnosis. These patients were usually misdiagnosed with major depression. Another study found that 50 percent of the men who were diagnosed with only drug or alcohol abuse should have also been diagnosed with BD. Other research indicates that 20–50 percent of patients diagnosed with schizophrenia during the 1970s actually suffered from BD.

Currently Overdiagnosed?

While BD seems to have been underdiagnosed in the past, many experts cite evidence that it is being overdiagnosed in the twenty-first century. Research published in 2010 in the *Journal of Clinical Psychiatry* found that almost 90 percent of children diagnosed with BD actually have other disorders such as attention deficit/hyperactivity disorder (ADHD) or conduct

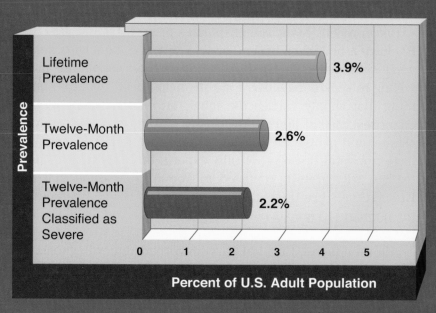

Prevalence of Bipolar Disorder

Twelve-Month Prevalence: 2.6% of U.S. adult population.

Severe: 82.9% of these cases (e.g., 2.2% of U.S. adult population) are classified as "severe."

Lifetime Prevalence: **3.9%**

Twelve-Month Prevalence: **2.6%**

Twelve-Month Prevalence Classified as Severe: **2.2%**

Prevalence

0   1   2   3   4   5

Percent of U.S. Adult Population

Taken from: National Institute of Mental Health. www.nimh.nih.gov/statistics/bipolar_adult_shtml.

disorder, which share some symptoms, such as high energy levels and rapid mood swings, with BD.

Mental health experts have called for revised diagnostic criteria to reduce the incidence of misdiagnosis. "What the new data on rates of diagnosis suggest is that many children may be misdiagnosed as bipolar because they don't fit neatly into the current diagnostic categories for emotional disorders,"[1] says psychiatrist Ellen Leibenluft of the NIMH in a *New York Times* article.

Other experts believe that increased awareness of BD among doctors has contributed to making it a catchall diagnosis for many mood and behavior disorders. In a 2010 letter to the editor of *Primary Psychiatry*, Dr. Roger Z. Samuel of the Boca Raton Psychiatric Group in Florida writes, "The rise in bipolar disorder rates reported in the US may be a local or regional trend, which is the 'flavor of the day' that is magnified by lax diagnostic thinking and precision."[2]

Samuel also suggests that one reason for the increases in BD diagnosis in the United States may have to do with drug companies' influencing of doctors to prescribe expensive new medications. "It is more than coincidence that this increase in awareness and rates of diagnosis of bipolar disorder in youths corresponds with the increase in the more expensive pharmaceutical interventions promoted by the pharmaceutical industry,"[3] he writes in his letter.

A Real Increase?

Another explanation for the increase in bipolar diagnosis is that more people truly have the disease. No one is sure why this may be true, but several theories have been proposed. Some doctors believe that the increased use of illegal drugs over the past fifty years is to blame. Many studies have shown that substance abuse is one factor that can trigger or worsen BD. A 2006 study at Mount Sinai Medical School in New York found that about 65 percent of the BD patients seen in the hospital were hospitalized shortly after abusing cocaine, marijuana, hallucinogens, or methamphetamine. No one has proven, however, that drug use accounts for the dramatic rise in BD cases.

Another theory is that a dramatic increase in the use of antidepressant medications is behind the rise in BD. While antidepressants are effective against unipolar depression, they often cause episodes of mania in depressed people who are actually bipolar. Thus, many people who never had a manic episode and would have been diagnosed with unipolar depression are now being diagnosed with BD because antidepressants revealed the disease.

Since biological, social, and environmental factors all play a role in causing BD, other experts have proposed that social changes coupled with an inborn predisposition may underlie

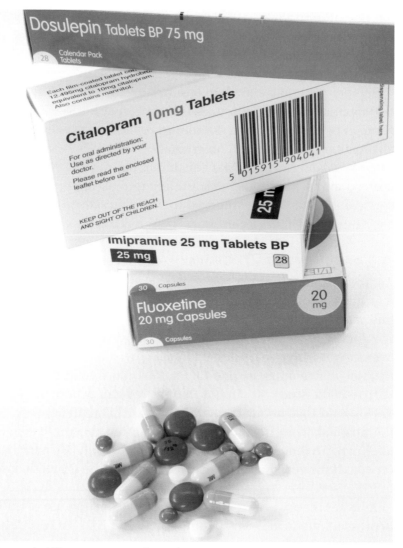

Several different types of antidepressant medication are available by prescription, and their use is on the rise. This trend may be linked to the increase in the number of people diagnosed with BD.

the increase in BD diagnoses. In a 2011 article in *Psychology Today*, psychiatrist Robert J. Hedaya of Georgetown University writes, "Early child rearing [in the United States] is more likely to be by a day care center—which is inherently unstable (people change centers or caregivers change in a center) and

impersonal. There is a higher likelihood of bullying and reduced supervision [than at home]. The result of this is impaired
social bonding in those who are particularly vulnerable."[4] This
type of stress, he states, can trigger BD directly or lead to
precipitating behaviors such as substance abuse. Hedaya also
believes that the overly processed foods that most Americans
now eat may lead to changes in brain chemistry that can trigger
BD. His theories have not been scientifically proven.

   Whatever the true causes for the increasing number of BD
cases may be, doctors and advocacy groups believe it is important to take action to understand and control this trend.
Bipolar disorder has a serious impact on individuals, families,
and society, and researchers are currently studying the factors
that may be responsible for the rise in cases. Other scientists
are attempting to gain a better understanding of the causes of
BD in hopes of learning how to prevent, more easily diagnose,
and provide better treatments for this increasingly common
disease.

CHAPTER ONE

What Is Bipolar Disorder?

Although it is known primarily as a mood disorder, bipolar disorder (BD) is a brain disease that affects an individual's thoughts, energy levels, and behavior as well as mood. Sometimes called by its previous official name of manic-depressive illness (or manic depression), BD is characterized by drastic shifts in all of these qualities. People in a manic state have high levels of energy, overly positive thoughts, and frantic behavior. In contrast, those who are depressed have negative thoughts, no energy, and difficulty getting anything accomplished. Everyone has some degree of ups and downs, but with BD these changes are extreme and interfere with everyday functioning. According to the National Institute of Mental Health (NIMH), "Bipolar disorder symptoms can result in damaged relationships, poor job or school performance, and even suicide."[5] Indeed, about 15 percent of BD patients take their own lives.

Medical historians believe BD has affected people throughout history, but no one is known to have related drastic shifts from mania to depression to a single disease until around A.D. 2 when the ancient Greek physician Aretaeus of Cappadocia wrote, "It appears to me that melancholy [depression] is the commencement [beginning] and a part of mania. . . . The development of mania is really a worsening of the disease rather than a change into another disease."[6]

The disease was not widely known until the late 1600s, nor did most experts link melancholy and mania into a single disease again until 1686, when the Swiss physician Theophile Bonet wrote about a condition he called "manico-melancolicus." After that, the disease had several other names prior to being given its present one. In 1854 the French doctor Jules Falret coined the term *folie circulaire* (circular insanity), and in 1896 the German psychiatrist Emil Kraepelin was the first to use the term *manic depression* in his textbook *Compendium der Psychiatrie*, where he wrote a detailed description and distinguished BD from schizophrenia. In 1980 psychiatrists who revised the *Diagnostic and Statistical Manual of Mental Disorders* (DSM) changed the official name to *bipolar disorder*.

Mood Episodes

As its name implies, the hallmark of BD is extreme shifts between the two "poles" of mania and depression. One patient describes these shifts as "I feel like a yo-yo on God's sick

People experiencing an episode of mania usually exhibit high levels of energy and activity, creativity, impulsiveness, and other behaviors that can disrupt their ability to function in their daily lives.

Bipolar Disorder Versus Personality Quirks

One factor that can make bipolar disorder difficult to diagnose is that many patients and those around them do not relate their symptoms to a serious disorder. In a *New York Times* article Dr. Richard A. Friedman explains how a failure to recognize danger signals played out for a patient named Bruce:

> No hurdle seemed too high or problem insolvable. . . . Betting that his future earnings would more than cover large expenses, he put off filing his state tax returns. . . . No one questioned his renewed energy and vigor [after a bout of depression] because he had always been vivacious. Nor did his combative behavior and ever increasing volume of provocative e-mail messages to friends and colleagues raise a suspicion that something might be seriously amiss. . . . No one seemed to recognize just how impaired his judgment had become. Even the judge who placed him on probation for failure to file tax returns missed the real story.

Richard A. Friedman, M.D. "When Bipolar Masquerades as a Happy Face." *New York Times*. www.nytimes.com/ref/health/healthguide/bipolar_ess.html.

string."[7] Doctors use the poles to further classify mood disorders as unipolar (one pole) or bipolar (two poles). People with unipolar disorders experience only one extreme mood state, usually depression, whereas those with bipolar disorder experience both extremes.

The degree and frequency of the mood and behavior shifts in BD vary widely among patients and within the same person at different times. In most cases, though, the disorder lasts a lifetime once it appears, with episodes of mania alternating with depression. It is thus considered to be a chronic disease.

As the NIMH explains, "Episodes of mania and depression typically come back over time. Between episodes, many people with bipolar disorder are free of symptoms, but some people may have lingering symptoms."[8]

Doctors assess the degree of mania or depression on a continuum, or scale, that ranges from normal to severe. The degree of depression ranges from mild to moderate to severe, or major, depression. People with mania may have severe mania on down to a condition called hypomania, which is characterized by increased energy levels, thoughts, and activity levels, but not to the extent seen in true mania.

Experts generally distinguish the degree of mania and depression by using standardized questionnaires to assess the impact of these states on an individual's ability to function. For example, the National Alliance on Mental Illness (NAMI) explains the distinction between hypomania and mania: "Mania typically causes obvious problems in daily functioning and often leads to serious problems with a person's relationships or work functioning. By definition, hypomania does not cause problems to the same extent as mania."[9] Less-intense emotional states such as hypomania, however, often progress to more severe episodes if untreated.

In addition to experiencing varying degrees of manic and depressive episodes, people with BD can also have symptoms of mania and depression at the same time. Doctors call these episodes mixed states.

Symptoms of Mania and Depression

Patients in a manic state report feeling energetic, "high," happy, outgoing, jumpy, irritable, invincible, and very creative. One woman describes her mania like this: "I feel like I have a motor attached. Everything is moving slowly, and I want to go, go, go. I feel like one of those toys that somebody winds up and sends spinning or doing cartwheels or whatever."[10]

Manic people may talk fast, have racing thoughts, and jump from one project or idea to another. They sleep little, party nonstop, and often launch ambitious projects because they believe they can accomplish anything they want to. Many do impulsive and risky things like quitting a job, spending a lot of money, having promiscuous sex, speeding in cars or motorcycles, running across rooftops, or jumping off a cliff because they believe they cannot get hurt. Some are angry and violent toward others or themselves. Yet people in a manic or hypomanic state are not likely to seek medical help because they think everything is wonderful and that they do not need help. Experts often refer to this as "the seductiveness of mania."

People in a depressed state, on the other hand, are more likely to seek help because they feel overwhelmingly sad, helpless, and hopeless. The individual's energy and grandiose plans evaporate, and debilitating tiredness sets in. The person may have trouble sleeping or may sleep most of the time. Many depressed people do not feel like getting out of bed at all. They lose interest in activities they once enjoyed and often shun all social contacts. Concentrating and making decisions becomes overwhelming. The person may eat too much or not enough and will frequently have unexplained aches and pains. Some depressed people attempt or commit suicide.

A twenty-four-year-old patient named Kaity describes her depression in a Depression and Bipolar Support Alliance article: "Overwhelming, consuming, shattering. . . . This grief is unnatural. This grief is unstoppable. Sometimes in depression, I can almost feel the claws of despair scoring the inside of my skin, lacerating what remains of me to make total room for the enemy."[11]

Patients with mixed states have elements of both mania and depression. They are often agitated and energetic, but also feel sad and have trouble sleeping. Those with mixed states, as well as with mania or depression, commonly abuse drugs and alcohol, which can worsen other symptoms of the disease.

Those in manic, depressive, or mixed states may also have psychotic symptoms, such as delusions (false beliefs) and hallucinations (false sensory perceptions, such as hearing voices). Delusions and hallucinations contribute to the inability to distinguish fantasy from reality that characterizes psychosis. The delusions an individual has seem to depend on whether he or she is manic or depressed. Thus, someone who is manic and

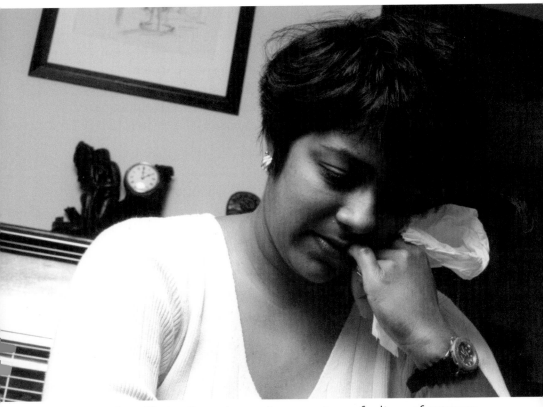

People suffering from depression experience feelings of extreme sadness, low energy, sleep disturbances, difficulty concentrating, and physical pain.

psychotic may falsely believe he is famous, wealthy, or has superpowers. A depressed psychotic patient may think she is a failure, a criminal, or destitute, regardless of the truth.

Although the specific symptoms of BD vary among individuals, the general characteristics of the disease are consistent, and have remained consistent, over time. Descriptions of symptoms by doctors today are remarkably similar to those by doctors throughout history. Aretaeus, for example, wrote,

> They with whose madness joy is associated, laugh, play, dance night and day, and sometimes go openly to the market crowned, as if victors in some contest of skill. . . . Others have madness attended with anger; and these

sometimes rend [rip] their clothes and kill their keepers, and lay violent hands upon themselves. . . . They are also given to extraordinary phantasies. . . . They are of a changeable temper, their senses are acute, they are suspicious, irritable without any cause, and unreasonably desponding [hopeless] when the disease tends to gloom.[12]

Symptoms in Children and Adolescents

The greatest differences in symptoms become apparent when comparing children and adolescents with BD with adults suffering from BD. According to the *Medifocus Guidebook on Bipolar Disorder*, "Onset of bipolar disorder during child-

Children with BD are often aggressive and prone to explosive temper tantrums.

hood and adolescence appears to be a more severe form of bipolar than adult onset and there tends to be more psychosis involved. . . . Children and adolescents also tend to experience very rapid mood swings many times a day. It is common to see children experience depressive states in the morning that is followed by increasing energy and mania later in the afternoon or evening."[13]

Adults too can experience rapidly shifting moods, known as rapid cycling, but rarely do these shifts occur daily as is often seen in children and teens. Young people with BD also tend to not have periods of recovery in between episodes. They may go for months or years with continuous illness.

The behaviors seen in youngsters with BD are also more likely to include explosive temper tantrums and aggression, as well as long bouts of crying. Then, the child may abruptly start laughing hysterically for no reason, which may last for only a while, followed by another bout of explosive anger.

Some of the extreme behaviors seen in children are specific to youth; for instance, a ten-year-old may announce that he is smarter than his teacher and will get up and try to teach his class at school. But some behaviors are inappropriate for the person's age. Many children, even small children with BD, act flirtatious and try to touch other people's genitals. And even though children typically need more sleep than adults do, youngsters with BD often sleep only four or five hours per night.

Not all children with BD have intense, constant symptoms. In some cases, those with mild depression or hypomania gradually worsen over time and go on to develop full-blown bipolar disorder later on. In other instances a child may have some symptoms of BD, but no one suspects that anything is really wrong. Family members may simply label the child as moody or socially withdrawn or as being a very energetic daredevil. As with adults, the boundaries between normal ups and downs and BD may be difficult to distinguish. If professional help is sought, the child (or adult) may or may not be diagnosed with

BD or may possibly be misdiagnosed with a disease that shares some characteristics with BD.

Difficulties in Diagnosis

The fact that BD can be mistaken for other disorders is one factor that can make diagnosis in people of any age difficult. According to the authors of *Living with Someone Who's Living with Bipolar Disorder*, "It has been estimated that the average bipolar patient suffers through *ten years* of symptoms before receiving a correct diagnosis."[14]

One of the illnesses that is most commonly misdiagnosed as BD (or vice versa) is attention deficit/hyperactivity disorder, or ADHD, which is characterized by hyperactivity, distractibility, an inability to concentrate, and sometimes rapid talking. Doctors distinguish BD from ADHD primarily by the fact that unlike ADHD, BD includes grandiose delusions, overt sexual behavior, elation, and a decreased need for sleep. ADHD also does not include alternating episodes of mania and depression. Sometimes, however, the symptoms of BD and ADHD are so similar that misdiagnosis occurs. The fact that 50–98 percent of children and adolescents with BD also have ADHD further complicates diagnosis. In such cases, making a dual diagnosis (diagnosing both disorders in the same person) can be especially challenging.

The fact that BD often occurs with several other disorders besides ADHD adds to the complexity of diagnosis. Experts estimate that over 70 percent of BD patients also have another mental illness. The most common is substance abuse; nearly 60 percent of people with BD abuse drugs and/or alcohol at some point. Other commonly co-occurring disorders are post-traumatic stress disorder, which follows a traumatic event like being in a war, and anxiety disorder.

Other disorders that are often confused with BD are antisocial personality disorder, conduct disorder, and borderline personality disorder. People with antisocial personality disorder or conduct disorder are sociopaths or psychopaths. They are self-centered, angry, manipulative, and without conscience, and they often abuse others and may even commit violent crimes such as murder. Unlike with BD, their behaviors are ongoing and do not respond to treatment. Borderline personality disorder also shares some qualities with BD, but is not episodic. Typically, people with borderline personality disorder are continuously impulsive, angry, and irritable. Sometimes its symptoms resemble those in rapid cycling BD, so it may be difficult for a doctor to distinguish which disorder a patient has.

Major depression and schizophrenia are also often misdiagnosed as BD or vice versa. Generally, if these disorders are observed by a professional over time, the distinctions between

Alcohol and drug abuse is a problem for nearly 60 percent of people who are diagnosed with BD.

Bipolar Diagnostic Criteria

Doctors diagnose bipolar disorder (BD) using criteria set out in the *Diagnostic and Statistical Manual of Mental Disorders*, now in its fourth edition (DSM-IV). In order to be diagnosed with one of the four main types of BD, a patient must satisfy the following criteria for different kinds of episodes, according to the DSM-IV:

1. Criteria for a manic episode include three or more of the following that last for at least one week (less if hospitalization is necessary):
   - Inflated self-esteem
   - Need little sleep
   - Unusually talkative
   - Racing thoughts
   - Easily distracted
   - Increased goal-directed activity
   - Engaging in risky activities such as sexual promiscuity, spending sprees, foolish business investments, or driving way too fast

them and BD become clearer. Most types of schizophrenia are characterized by delusions and hallucinations more than by extreme emotional moods; however, one disorder (schizoaffective disorder), which is closely related to schizophrenia, is sort of a cross between schizophrenia and BD, and it is often very difficult for a doctor to distinguish it from BD.

With major depression, misdiagnosis most often occurs when a patient with BD sees a doctor only during depressive episodes. Andy Behrman, author of *Electroboy: A Memory of Mania,* had this experience:

For more than ten years, I was consistently misdiagnosed with depression by more than eight mental health care pro-

2. Criteria for hypomania include three or more of the symptoms of mania that last at least four days but do not require hospitalization; do not lead to significant difficulties at school, work, or in social relationships; and do not involve psychosis.

3. Criteria for a major depressive episode include five or more of the following over two weeks:
   - Depressed mood most of the day, nearly every day, including tearfulness, sadness, or irritability
   - Feeling no pleasure and diminished interest in activities
   - Significant weight loss or weight gain and increase or decrease in appetite
   - Inability to sleep or sleeping too much
   - Slowed behavior
   - Fatigue and loss of energy
   - Feelings of worthlessness or inappropriate guilt
   - Inability to concentrate and make decisions
   - Recurrent thoughts of death or suicide, or attempted suicide

fessionals. . . . In a nutshell, I was being diagnosed improperly because I only visited these doctors during my "low points" or depression; I was not accurately filling them in on my symptoms, and they were not asking enough questions about my mental illness. In retrospect, had I shared more information with them perhaps it would have been easier for them to diagnose me with bipolar disorder.[15]

The Diagnostic Process

Difficulties in making an accurate diagnosis is one factor that contributes to the often lengthy diagnostic process that begins when a person seeks help from a medical professional. The doctor will conduct a physical examination, order laboratory tests, take a medical history, and have the patient complete a standardized mental evaluation and questionnaires to help with diagnosis. There are no obvious physical or biochemical signs of bipolar disorder, but a physical exam, blood tests, and imaging tests can help the physician rule out other disorders, such as a brain tumor, that might be contributing to the patient's symptoms. The medical history will tell the doctor about the person's family history of mental illness, which can play a role in increasing the likelihood of BD, and about the individual's previous medical problems. If a doctor is reason-

After having ruled out any physical reasons as the cause of symptoms of BD, a doctor will often refer a patient to a psychiatrist, who then makes a diagnosis based upon a standard set of criteria.

ably sure that the patient has a mental disorder such as BD, he or she will generally make a referral to a psychiatrist (medical doctor who specializes in mental diseases).

The specialist or family doctor bases a diagnosis of BD on criteria set forth in the *Diagnostic and Statistical Manual of Mental Disorders*, which specifies four basic types of the disease. The first type, Bipolar I disorder, is the most severe and typical form. Patients have severe manic episodes, and usually depressive episodes as well, that differ significantly from previous behavior. Manic or mixed episodes must last at least seven days (less if hospitalization is required) and depressive episodes at least two weeks. Symptoms must include at least three in a list of characteristic behaviors and must be severe enough to cause noticeable difficulties at home, school, or work. Symptoms may be serious enough that the patient requires hospitalization to prevent harm to oneself or others.

Bipolar II disorder is less severe than Bipolar I and is characterized by depressive episodes alternating with hypomania, but no full-blown mania or mixed episodes. People with both Bipolar I and II may also be diagnosed with rapid cycling. This involves having four or more episodes of major depression, mania, hypomania, or mixed states within one year.

Doctors diagnose the third type of BD, Bipolar disorder not otherwise specified, when a person's symptoms do not last long enough to qualify as Bipolar I or II but are clearly different than the individual's normal behavior.

The fourth type, cyclothymic disorder, or cyclothymia, is the mildest form of BD. It includes episodes of hypomania that alternate with mild depression for at least two years for adults and one year for children and adolescents. The criteria for other types of BD are not met with this diagnosis.

Whatever type of bipolar disorder a person has, it generally worsens over time without treatment. Thus, doctors emphasize that obtaining an accurate diagnosis as soon as possible is important for helping to prevent increased frequency and severity of episodes. Many patients, though, wait for many years before seeking help, and the consequences can be devastating. As one man writes, "I've always had mood swings. I used to throw huge tantrums when I was a kid. As I got older, the highs got higher and the lows got lower. I lost several jobs and ruined a whole bunch of relationships. Finally, I decided nothing could be worse than living like I was, and I went to get some help."[16]

The symptoms and diagnosis of BD are not the only things about the disorder that are complex. The causes too are complicated and involve diverse interactions among many factors.

CHAPTER TWO

What Causes Bipolar Disorder?

Doctors have held different views about the causes of bipolar disorder (BD) throughout history. The ancient Greek physician Aretaeus believed the disorder resulted from "want of purgation of the system."[17] The accumulation of waste materials in the body, Aretaeus wrote, led to problems with the brain. Aretaeus and others during his era also believed that a body fluid they called yellow bile played a role in causing depression and mania. Although these doctors were wrong about the specific physical abnormalities that underlie BD, they were accurate in surmising that some mental illnesses can have biological causes.

Later, during the Middle Ages, most people, including doctors, thought demons or witches caused mental illnesses. In the 1600s some experts began to realize that the ancient Greek idea that physical abnormalities could contribute to mental illnesses was more accurate than was the theory that supernatural forces were to blame.

In the late nineteenth century the German psychiatrist Emil Kraepelin proposed that genes were responsible for BD, and in the twentieth century Sigmund Freud, who founded the psychoanalytic school of psychiatry, put forth the view that manic depression resulted from traumatic early experiences and lasting psychological conflicts. Later in his career, however, Freud adjusted his beliefs and stated that manic depression probably resulted more from biological abnormalities in the brain than from emotional trauma. He reached this conclusion because he found that attempts to treat the disease with psychotherapy were ineffective.

Complex Interactions

Modern doctors have good evidence that Freud's later opinion about the causes of BD and Kraepelin's genetic hypothesis are accurate. Freud's earlier opinion that traumatic events can play a role has also been shown to be valid. Experts now know that BD results from complex interactions between biological, social, and environmental factors. According to the National Institute of Mental Health (NIMH), "Most scientists agree that there is no single cause. Rather, many factors likely act together to produce the illness or increase risk."[18]

No one is certain about precisely which combinations of biological, social, and environmental factors cause BD, but experts do know that having family members with the disease, having a great deal of stress in one's life, abusing drugs and alcohol, and being between fifteen and thirty years old are some of the main risk factors that increase an individual's likelihood of developing the illness.

The finding that having a family history of BD significantly raises the risk of getting the disease has led scientists to conclude that genes play a causal role. Genes are the parts of DNA (deoxyribonucleic acid) molecules that pass hereditary information from parents to their offspring. Genes reside on worm-shaped bodies called chromosomes in the center of each body cell. The sequence of chemicals that compose genes encodes a set of instructions telling the cell how to operate and produce essential proteins.

Genetic information and gene mutations (abnormalities) can be passed directly or inherited as a predisposition. Examples of genetic traits that are passed on directly include hair color, eye color, and diseases such as cystic fibrosis. Individuals who inherit a single gene or mutation for these qualities show cer-

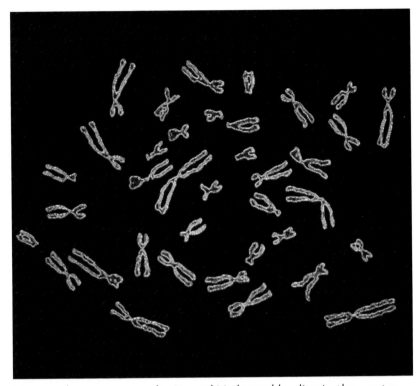

Human chromosomes, the X- and Y-shaped bodies in the center of each cell, contain genes that determine specific human traits and characteristics, including diseases. Scientists have determined that BD can have a genetic basis.

tain characteristics or develop certain diseases regardless of environmental events.

In contrast, multiple genes or mutations contribute to a genetic predisposition, or tendency, and the inherited traits will not become apparent unless triggering environmental events are also present. Scientists believe a genetic predisposition is involved in causing bipolar disorder.

Evidence for a Genetic Cause

One piece of evidence that led scientists to conclude that a genetic predisposition plays a role in causing BD is that the disease tends to run in certain families. Children who have a parent or sibling with BD are four to six times likelier than

Brain Imaging Techniques

Modern technology allows doctors to study the structure and activity of the brain. This helps them determine which abnormalities underlie diseases such as bipolar disorder. Often-used technologies include the following:

- Magnetic resonance imaging (MRI) uses radio waves and magnetic fields to generate computer images of structures in the brain. It uses no radiation and provides more detailed images of soft tissue than computerized tomography (CT) does but is more expensive than the latter.
- Functional magnetic resonance imaging (fMRI) is similar to MRI, but uses technology that measures blood flow to gauge brain activity rather than structure, in certain areas. An fMRI is faster than a positron-emission tomography (PET) scan.
- Magnetic resonance spectroscopy (MRS) uses magnetic fields to measure brain chemicals and is useful in assessing and diagnosing the biochemical causes of some diseases.
- Computerized tomography/computerized axial tomography (CT/CAT) uses X-rays to create cross-sectional computer-generated pictures of the brain. CT/CAT provides much more detail than conventional X-rays do.

other children to develop the disorder. When both parents have BD, a child's risk increases by 50 to 75 percent. Other aspects of the disease, such as the age at which the first manic episode occurs and the number and frequency of episodes, are also consistent within families.

Studies of identical twins, who share identical genes, have also proved a genetic link. When one twin has BD, the other twin also has it 60 to 80 percent of the time. Nonidentical, or fraternal, twins, who share only about 50 percent of their genes, both have BD about 20 percent of the time. "That tells us that about two-thirds of the risk for bipolar disorder can be explained by genes,"[19] says Dr. Francis J. McMahan of NIMH.

- PET uses radioactive tracers injected into a blood vessel to measure brain structure and function, such as blood flow, oxygen use, and metabolism. The PET scanner detects and records the energy given off by the tracer, and a computer converts this information into three-dimensional pictures. Unlike MRI and CT, PET can detect minute cellular changes.

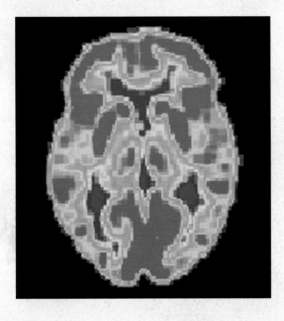

A PET scan is one example of several types of brain imaging techniques.

Scientists have also determined that several gene mutations are linked to BD. Not all people with the disease have each mutation, and investigators believe more genes that contribute to a predisposition to develop the disease will be found as well.

Researchers identify genes linked to a particular disease by studying the genome (the complete DNA signature) of people with and without the disorder. High-tech molecular genetic laboratory techniques such as polymerase chain reaction allow identification and sequencing of gene patterns. Computer tools such as the Bipolar Disorder Phenome Database, which links symptoms with genes that may cause these symptoms, also assist scientists in this quest.

Thus far, several teams of researchers have linked abnormalities in certain genes that govern the production and regulation of brain chemicals, or neurotransmitters, such as serotonin, norepinephrine, dopamine, and glutamate to BD. These chemicals all contribute to mood, energy levels, and thought processes. One such gene is the human serotonin transporter gene, which is important in regulating mood and sleep. Defects in genes that regulate calcium and sodium channels, or gates, on the surface of nerve cells have also been shown to play a role in BD. The Akyrin3 and CACNA1C genes, for example, determine whether or not a nerve cell, or neuron, will let certain brain chemicals flow in or out. This in

Identical twins share identical genes. Scientists have found that when one twin has BD, the other twin has a 60 to 80 percent chance of having the disease as well.

turn determines whether or not the neuron will fire and pass along messages to other neurons. Researchers have linked the abnormal nerve firing that results from defective Akyrin3 and CACNA1C to the development of BD.

Mutations in a gene called CLOCK are also linked to BD. People with these mutations are especially likely to experience relapses (recurrences) of episodes following inadequate sleep. The CLOCK gene influences the internal biological clock, which consists of mechanisms in the suprachiasmatic nucleus of the hypothalamus in the brain that govern sleep and wakefulness cycles. Researchers believe that people with BD "may have a molecular clock that is unable to properly adapt to changes in the environment,"[20] writes psychiatrist C.A. McClung of the University of Texas Southwestern Medical Center. Further evidence that disruptions in biological rhythms are involved in causing BD comes from studies showing that people with the disease are likely to have more depressive episodes in winter and more manic episodes in summer. The biological clock is influenced by seasonal variations in daylight.

Discoveries of other mutations linked to BD as well as to other mental disorders indicate that genes that govern the development of psychotic symptoms and the brain's response to some drugs play a role in determining a genetic predisposition to multiple mental illnesses. Scientists believe the particular pattern of mutations may determine which disease an individual develops. In September 2011, for example, researchers at the Mount Sinai School of Medicine in New York reported that they found eleven gene mutations that increase the risk of developing both BD and schizophrenia. Other scientists have identified gene mutations that occur in people with BD and alcoholism.

Brain Abnormalities

The genetic defects that underlie BD in turn result in abnormal brain activity and structure that directly contribute to causing the disorder. Brain imaging techniques such as magnetic resonance imaging (MRI), functional magnetic resonance imaging

Theories About What Causes Rapid Cycling

Medical experts believe multiple causes probably underlie rapid cycling in bipolar disorder (BD). No one has proven what these causes are, but several hypotheses have been put forth, including the following:

1. One theory is the kindling theory. This theory proposes that early episodes of BD are triggered by stressful major life events in biologically susceptible people. Over time, the patient becomes increasingly sensitive to stressful minor events and eventually continues to have episodes even when no stressful triggers are present.

2. The biological rhythm disturbance theory proposes that people with rapid cycling have abnormal biological clocks that get more and more abnormal over time. Thus, the patient's sleep and waking cycles are increasingly irregular, and this may contribute to increasingly frequent and serious bipolar episodes.

3. The hypothyroidism hypothesis proposes that rapid cycling results from inadequate levels of thyroid hormone in the brain, even when blood thyroid levels are normal. Several studies have found that people who experience rapid cycling have low thyroid levels in the brain while other studies have found no such link. Thus, this hypothesis remains controversial.

(fMRI), magnetic resonance spectroscopy (MRS), and positron-emission tomography (PET) allow doctors to take pictures and study brain chemicals and activity inside the brain.

Many studies have shown that the brains of people with BD differ from those of healthy people and from those with other mental disorders. According to the authors of *Living with Someone Who's Living with Bipolar Disorder*, "Unlike many brain disorders—such as a tumor or stroke—BD is not localized to one part of the brain. It involves abnormalities of several regions or diffuse [scattered] functions."[21]

Structural abnormalities in the brains of BD patients include decreased size and cell density in the anterior cingulate cortex, prefrontal cortex, and hippocampus. These areas are all involved in regulating thoughts and emotions, and they show abnormal activity as well as structural abnormalities. For instance, scientists have linked diminished activity and abnormal firing between neurons in the right prefrontal cortex with symptoms of mania.

An illustration shows the location of the amygdala in the human brain (the two highlighted areas). The amygdala has been shown to respond to emotional triggers for BD.

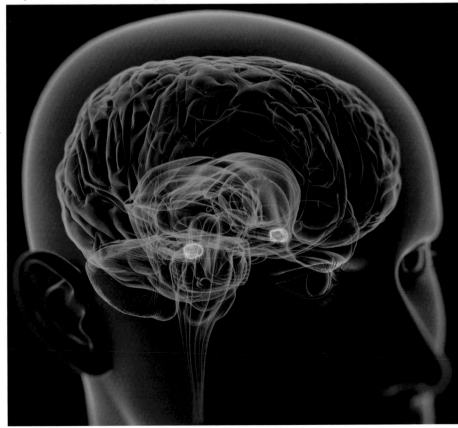

Another brain area called the amygdala also appears to play a role in causing BD. As psychiatrist Ellen Leibenluft of the NIMH explains, "The amygdala tells us what in our environment is emotionally important. It seems to be acting differently in bipolar disorder, in both adults and children. We see an increased activity in the amygdala in response to emotional triggers in the environment."[22]

Recent research indicates that some of the abnormal brain activity seen in people with BD may result from altered synapses and nerve cell plasticity (the ability of neural circuits to change). Synapses are tiny gaps between neurons. Neurons communicate with each other by sending chemical and electrical signals across these synapses. Signals are sent by long nerve cell extensions called axons and received by receptors on shorter branches called dendrites.

Several researchers cite evidence that some gene mutations associated with BD produce abnormal activity in synapses. This in turn is associated with defects in nerve plasticity, which is essential for normal brain operations. Plasticity allows the brain to adapt to internal and external conditions. One cell part that regulates plasticity is the mitochondrion, or cell powerhouse. Studies have shown that defects in cell energy production lead to altered synapses and plasticity. Scientists believe therefore that BD results at least partly from an inability of brain cells and circuits to communicate and adapt to changing conditions. Researchers are currently attempting to gain a better understanding of how these processes work in hopes of further untangling the complex biological causes of BD.

The Role of Sex Hormones

Many experts believe that sex hormones also play a role in causing the brain changes that underlie BD. They have reached this conclusion because most cases of the disease begin during adolescence and young adulthood, when sex hormones become active. The relationship between sex hormones and BD, however, is not yet clear. Scientists do know

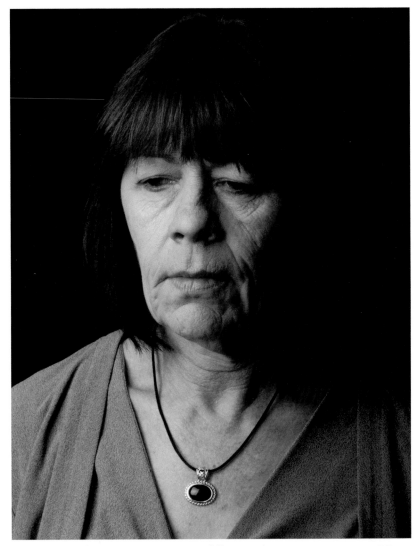

The onset of menopause in a middle-aged woman can cause BD symptoms, particularly depression, to become worse.

that sex hormones affect the brain in various ways. Estrogen, the primary female hormone, enhances the activity of the neurotransmitters serotonin, norepinephrine, dopamine, and gamma-aminobutyric acid (GABA) in the brain. Furthermore, menopause, when a middle-aged woman stops menstruating, is characterized by dramatic decreases in estrogen levels and is associated with worsening symptoms of BD, particularly depression. A study at the University of California at its Berkeley and Davis campuses also showed that after menopause, women who do not take estrogen supplements have less activity in several areas of the cerebral cortex and smaller volume in the hippocampus compared with women who do take these supplements.

Further connections between estrogen and the brain emerge from the fact that many women experience mood swings right before they start to menstruate each month, but scientists are not sure why this happens and are currently conducting studies to evaluate what factors may influence which women are prone to these premenstrual symptoms. Other research indicates that women who take birth control pills have larger areas of gray matter in the prefrontal cortex, pre- and post-central gyri, hippocampus, and temporal regions of the brain compared with women who do not take these drugs. Birth control pills add female hormones to the natural mix and also lower levels of naturally occurring hormones, but again, experts are unsure of what the underlying mechanisms behind the effects on the brain may be.

Studies reported in 2010 and 2011 in the *Journal of Neuroscience* show that estrogen receptors on neurons influence the structure and activity of synapses in the brain, and these findings may offer clues as to how estrogen influences mood. But none of these studies provide answers to how and why BD is likely to begin during adolescence and young adulthood. Scientists are now conducting other studies to shed more light on this issue.

There have been fewer studies examining the relationship between male hormones called androgens and BD, but scientists do know that when androgens such as testosterone become active during adolescence, this results in changes in brain circuits and structure. For instance, testosterone makes nerve fibers in the frontal lobes of the brain acquire more insulation during adolescence in males, and this allows faster signal transmission. The amygdala and hippocampus both increase in size at this time too, and scientists believe these changes may contribute to adolescents' increased vulnerability to BD.

Environmental Triggers

A genetic predisposition and subsequent biological abnormalities will not lead to BD unless other triggering events are present. Some of the events experts believe are involved are physical, emotional, or sexual abuse, particularly during childhood; sleep disruptions; and drug or alcohol abuse. Scientists, however, have not proved that any of these factors actually cause BD, as asserted by the author of *The Bipolar Disorder Survival Guide*:

> The hypothesis that a person's genetic inheritance or biological vulnerabilities interact with specific environmental conditions to produce bipolar disorder is just that—a hypothesis. To test this hypothesis in a research study, we would have to determine whether children born with a genetic history of bipolar disorder and affected by predisposing environmental conditions are more likely to develop bipolar disorder in adulthood than children with a similar genetic history who have not been affected by these environmental conditions. These long-term studies, which would take many years to complete and are extremely difficult to execute, have not been done.[23]

Although no specific events have been proved to cause BD, scientists do have strong evidence that several raise the risk significantly. A 2007 study showed that as many as 70 percent of patients experiencing their first manic episode do so during or shortly after abusing drugs or alcohol. Other studies indicate that people with BD who continue to abuse these substances have more frequent and severe episodes and are more likely to experience mixed states and rapid cycling.

Stressful events, or life changes that experts refer to as social rhythm disruptions, like a death or illness in the

Environmental factors, including positive life changes such as getting married or having a baby, can trigger BD, possibly because the brains of those with the condition are unable to manage their behavioral activation and inhibition systems.

family, a divorce, or abuse, can also trigger or worsen BD in biologically vulnerable people. A patient named Laurie, for example, writes, "I may have had the propensity for mental illness, but I believe I became ill as a result of the humiliation, shame, and abuse I suffered. My parents took everything I was away from me."[24] Laurie's adoptive parents and siblings sexually abused and beat her for many years. Doctors believe such stressors can trigger BD by increasing the body's production of chemicals such as the antistress hormone cortisol, which then acts to disrupt brain chemistry.

Researchers have found that even positive life changes, such as getting a job promotion, getting married, or having a baby can also trigger BD. One doctor who has studied this process extensively is psychology professor Sheri Johnson of the University of California at Berkeley. Johnson believes inborn abnormalities in parts of the brain that regulate emotional control and planning make the brains of people with BD unable to calm neural circuits known as the behavioral activation and inhibition systems. This lack of control occurs during both positive and negative life changes and can lead to manic or depressive episodes.

Johnson has also proposed that in some cases bipolar episodes cause life changes, which then trigger more bipolar episodes, in an ongoing spiral of events. For instance, an individual in a manic state may become belligerent at work and get fired from his job, which in turn intensifies the manic episode. The patient and his doctors may think the job loss triggered the manic episode, when in reality the mania caused the job loss. Ongoing research in this vein indicates that the interactions between life events and BD may be far more complicated than simple cause-and-effect relationships.

Another known trigger of BD episodes is sleep disruption. Patients report that even one night of going to bed late or getting up early can have serious consequences, leading to rapid cycling or worsening of manic or depressive symptoms. Doctors believe this happens because abnormalities in the biological clock make it difficult for patients to adapt to changing sleep patterns. Many times, life changes such as going off to college, getting married, starting a new relationship, or having a baby disrupt a person's sleep schedule, and the combination of changing events and sleep loss can cause BD to emerge or worsen.

The complex interactions between life events, genetics, and biochemistry that contribute to causing BD make pinning down the necessary and sufficient causes difficult. Different triggers affect different people in various ways, and ongoing research is attempting to understand what biological factors underlie these differences in individual responses. As scientists understand more and more about these processes, new and better treatments emerge, and experts hope that someday this understanding will also lead to methods of preventing the disease in vulnerable people.

CHAPTER THREE

How Is Bipolar Disorder Treated?

Like its causes and diagnosis, treatment of bipolar disorder (BD) is complex. Since the causes involve biological, social, and environmental factors, effective treatments focus on all of these variables. Different therapies and combinations of therapies work best for different patients, but in general, some combination of medication and psychotherapy is most effective. Oftentimes, finding the best types and dosages of medication and an ideal balance of other therapies can take months or even years.

It took many centuries for doctors to understand enough about BD for effective treatments to be developed. Throughout history the recommended treatments reflected prevailing views about the causes of the disease. For example, the ancient Greek physician Aretaeus was among the first to recognize that BD has a biological basis, and he recommended that patients drink spring water as a treatment. It turns out that spring water contains lithium, which is one of the primary modern treatment drugs for BD, so Aretaeus was accurate in his assessment that chemical compounds could effectively treat mental disorders. It was not until the twentieth century, however, that scientists developed actual medications to use in treatment.

During the Middle Ages and beyond, when many people attributed mental illnesses to demonic possession, accepted treatments included exorcism, torture, or simply restraining patients in asylums. Some psychiatrists after the 1600s tried using various chemicals as treatments but rarely achieved any success. In the early twentieth century Sigmund Freud introduced the idea of treating mental disorders with psychotherapy (talk therapy), and later on doctors began effectively using different forms of psychotherapy combined with certain drugs. Sometimes other therapies such as electroconvulsive therapy were, and are still, used as well.

Controversies Over Involuntary Treatment

There is a great deal of controversy over laws that mandate hospitalization or ongoing outpatient treatment for bipolar patients who do not want to be treated. Laws such as New York City's Kendra's Law, which was passed after a schizophrenic man who refused to take his prescribed medications pushed a woman named Kendra under a subway train, allow courts to order nonhospitalized mental patients to comply with treatment to protect the public.

Proponents of such laws, such as psychiatrist E. Fuller Torrey of the University of Health Sciences in Bethesda, Maryland, argue that involuntary treatment is needed in some cases for several reasons in addition to public protection from violent people. He writes,

> Scientifically, it has been shown in many recent studies that 40% to 50% of individuals with schizophrenia and bipolar disorder have an impaired awareness of their illness. . . . On humane grounds, the failure to treat such individuals often leads to homelessness or incarceration. . . . On humane grounds alone, is it fair to leave those who are not aware of their own illness living in the streets and eating out of garbage cans, as over 25% of the population with severe mental illness do?

Although BD is not curable, modern treatments help many patients recover from episodes and remain symptom-free for varying lengths of time. But in order for treatment to be effective, it must be ongoing. As Dr. David Miklowitz, the author of *The Bipolar Disorder Survival Guide*, explains, "The nature of bipolar disorder is such that even when you feel better, you still have an underlying biological predisposition to the illness. This predisposition requires you to take medication even when

Opponents of such laws argue that they infringe on the civil rights of the mentally ill and make these individuals less likely to voluntarily take medication in the future. Legal rights advocate Judi Chamberlain writes, "The issue here is not the use of psychiatric medications per se, but whether doctors should be permitted to force medications on unwilling recipients. . . . It is clear that the people under discussion have chosen not to be patients."

Quoted in the National Empowerment Center. "Should Forced Medication Be a Treatment Option in Patients with Schizophrenia?" www.power2u.org/debate.html.

A psychiatric nurse speaks to a patient in a hospital. Doctors, lawmakers, and advocates struggle to determine how best to deal with mentally ill people who refuse to treat their conditions.

you're feeling well."[25] The 2007 STEP-BD study funded by the National Institute of Mental Health (NIMH) found that ongoing treatment significantly reduces the number and severity of relapses, and patients who work closely with a psychiatrist and keep the doctor apprised of any mood changes so appropriate dosage or drug changes can be made have the best outcomes. Many patients find that keeping a daily mood chart or journal to track symptoms is especially helpful in managing an ongoing treatment plan.

Drug Treatments

The primary goal of drug therapy is to correct the chemical imbalances that underlie BD. Different drugs and combinations of drugs work best for different patients, and an individual's response to these medications can change over time, so ongoing monitoring is essential. Another factor that makes finding the right treatment plan an ongoing and complex process, says Miklowitz, is that "doctors have to be constantly updated on which treatments to recommend to which patients, since the accepted treatment guidelines for this disorder change so rapidly."[26]

Most patients require drug treatments for both acute (sudden) episodes and ongoing maintenance control. The medications or dosages used for each of these phases may vary. Ongoing treatment is usually administered on an outpatient basis, while acute episodes may require hospitalization with powerful, fast-acting drugs to stabilize the individual so he can function.

Most of the time, a patient voluntarily enters a psychiatric hospital or goes for outpatient treatment. But if the patient is an immediate danger to herself or others or has already committed a crime, a judge can mandate hospitalization or outpatient treatment. State laws vary on this issue, and some states allow family members and law enforcement personnel more leeway in forcing treatment on someone who does not want it. This is a controversial subject since balancing an individual's right to make his own decisions with the public's right to be safe from violent people with mental illness who refuse to take medication can be challenging.

Mood Stabilizers

The most common medications used for both acute episodes and ongoing therapy are mood stabilizers. Lithium (brand names Eskalith and Lithobid) is the oldest effective mood stabilizer; it was approved in 1970 for use in the United States. It works by stabilizing the biological clock and by slowing down message transmission between certain neurons. Recent research indicates that it may also slow the death of neurons in areas of the brain associated with BD.

Lithium, approved for use in the United States in 1970, is the oldest effective mood stabilizing medication; it is taken by about 60 percent of patients with BD despite its unpleasant side effects.

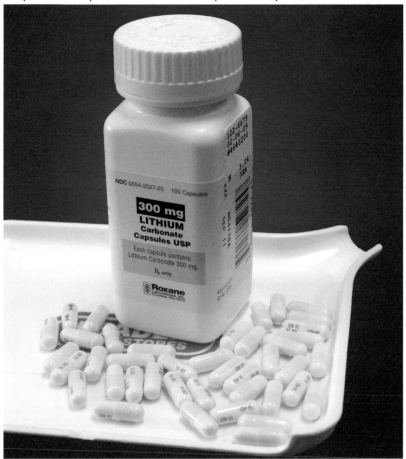

The Discovery of Lithium Treatment

Lithium was not only the first mood stabilizer to be approved for the treatment of bipolar disorder (BD), it was also the first effective psychiatric drug to be manufactured by drug companies. The Australian psychiatrist John Cade (1912–1980) first discovered and documented lithium's effectiveness in 1949, when he was working at a war veterans hospital near Melbourne. While studying the causes of BD, Cade hypothesized that a toxic chemical found in the urine of people with the disease might be at fault. In a 1947 article in the *Medical Journal of Australia* he wrote that mania was "a state of intoxication of a normal product of the body circulating in excess" and that "melancholia is the corresponding deprivative [deficiency] condition." In experiments designed to search for the toxic chemical, he injected guinea pigs with the urine of manic, depressed, and healthy people and found that the animals injected with urine from manic patients died much faster than the other animals did. Further experiments revealed that something in the part of the urine called urea was producing the toxic effects, and Cade began testing various compounds to reduce the toxicity.

He found that a form of lithium called lithium urate not only achieved this goal, but also calmed the guinea pigs. Cade later tried other forms of lithium such as lithium citrate and lithium carbonate. Lithium carbonate turned out to be most effective. Cade realized that this compound might have positive effects in people with BD, and he initially tried lithium carbonate on himself to make sure it was safe. He then tested it on patients and found that it produced dramatic improvements in those in a manic state.

Quoted in Philip B. Mitchell and Dusan Hadzi-Pavlovic. "Lithium Treatment for Bipolar Disorder." World Health Organization *Bulletin*, vol. 78, no. 4, 2000. www.who.int/bulletin/archives/78(4)515.pdf.

Lithium is effective in about 60 percent of patients, but it rarely helps those with rapid cycling, mixed states, or co-occurring substance abuse. NAMI states that "it generally has more positive impact when used earlier, rather than later, in the course of bipolar disorder."[27] Lithium is also far more effective in reducing the number of manic episodes than it is in treating depression, but it is widely prescribed because it is the only BD drug proven to reduce the risk of suicide.

One of the greatest drawbacks of lithium, as well as other drugs used to treat BD, is that it has unpleasant side effects. These may include seizures, hallucinations, restlessness, dry mouth, thirst, bloating, indigestion, acne, joint and muscle pain, brittle hair and nails, tremors, frequent urination, memory problems, loss of coordination, and kidney or thyroid damage. Doctors must carefully monitor blood levels of patients taking lithium to ensure that the dose is high enough to be therapeutic, but not so high as to cause the more dangerous side effects. The drug can also cause birth defects or heart problems in a developing fetus if taken by a pregnant woman, but experts say it is the safest BD medication to use during pregnancy if medication is essential in a given case.

Many patients stop taking lithium because of the side effects; about 30 percent of those who try it find it intolerable. Doctors emphasize that oftentimes the side effects are temporary and that a dosage adjustment can also reduce them, so they urge patients to discuss any concerns before stopping the medication.

Other mood stabilizers used to treat BD are anticonvulsant drugs originally developed to treat epilepsy. Valproic acid, also known as valproate or divalproex (Depakote) is the most widely used in this class. It works by reducing activity of the enzyme known as protein kinase C and increasing the activity of the neurotransmitter GABA, which calms neuron firing. Studies indicate that valproate is as effective as lithium for treating acute mania and is even more effective against rapid cycling and mixed states. Also, more patients find that they tolerate valproate better than lithium. For some patients, combining valproate and lithium works best.

Side effects of valproate may include drowsiness, dizziness, diarrhea, constipation, heartburn, runny nose, and liver or pancreas problems. It can also raise levels of the male hormone testosterone in both sexes, and this can lead to polycystic ovary syndrome (PCOS) in women who begin taking the drug before age twenty. PCOS involves a woman's eggs turning into fluid-filled cysts that can disrupt menstruation and lead to obesity and excess body hair.

Other anticonvulsants approved to treat BD include lamotrigine (Lamictal), gabapentin (Neurontin), topiramate (Topamax), carbamazepine (Tegretol), and oxcarbazepine (Trileptal). These are usually less effective than lithium or valproate but do help many patients who cannot tolerate the latter drugs. In addition, studies performed in 2003, 2004, and 2009 have shown lamotrigine to be more effective than lithium in preventing depressive relapses, rapid cycling, and mixed states.

All these anticonvulsants can cause drowsiness, nausea, blurry vision, memory loss, loss of coordination, and liver disease. In addition, all carry a warning that they may increase suicidal thoughts and can cause a life-threatening rash called Stevens-Johnson syndrome.

Other Medications

It may seem logical that using antidepressants along with mood stabilizers would be effective in treating BD, but this is often not the case. In general, antidepressants are not nearly as effective in helping depressed bipolar patients as they are for treating unipolar depression. A 2007 study reported in the *New England Journal of Medicine* found "no evidence that treatment with a mood stabilizer and an antidepressant confers a benefit over treatment with a mood stabilizer alone."[28] Other studies, however, have found that antidepressants can help manage depressive episodes far better than mood stabilizers do, so there is controversy among doctors about whether or not to prescribe antidepressants for BD. The fact that some antidepressants trigger mania in depressed BD patients also makes many physicians hesitate to prescribe them. Some stud-

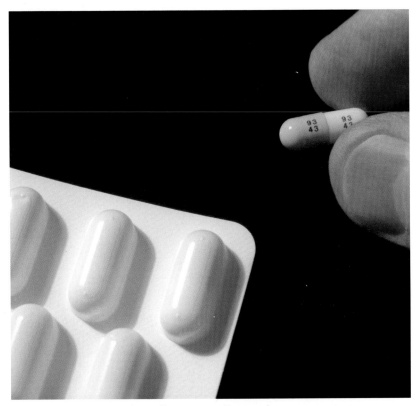

Antidepressants such as fluoxetine (Prozac) are sometimes prescribed to patients with BD to help them manage their depressive episodes, but it has been found to trigger mania in some people.

ies have concluded that antidepressants trigger mania only when they are used by themselves in bipolar patients, while other studies have found that this can happen when they are used along with mood stabilizers.

When they are used, antidepressants known as selective serotonin reuptake inhibitors (SSRIs), including fluoxetine (Prozac), paroxetine (Paxil), and sertraline (Zoloft), are among the most popular. Also frequently prescribed are serotonin-norepinephrine reuptake inhibitors (SNRIs), which act on both of these neurotransmitters. These include venlafaxine (Effexor) and duloxetine (Cymbalta). Older antidepressants called tricyclic antidepressants and monoamine oxidase inhibitors

Treatment/Services Used by Patients with Bipolar Disorder

Twelve-Month Health Care Use: 48.8% of those with the disorder are receiving treatment.

Percent Receiving Minimally Adequate Treatment: 38.8% of those receiving treatment are receiving minimally adequate treatment (18.8% of those with disorder).

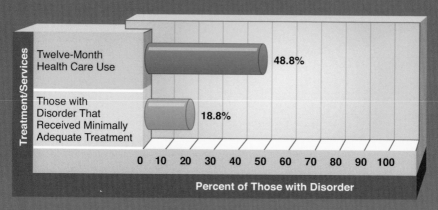

Twelve-Month Any Service Use, Including Health Care: 55.5% of those with the disorder are receiving treatment.

Percent Received Minimally Adequate Treatment: 39.2% of those receiving minimally adequate treatment (21.8% of those with disorder).

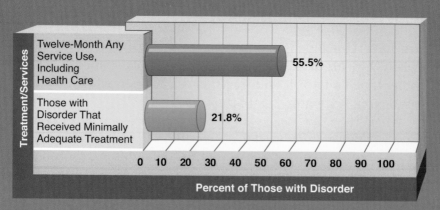

Taken from: National Institute of Mental Health. www.nimh.nih.gov/statistics/bipolar_adult_shtml.

(MAOIs) are also effective for some patients. All antidepressants can cause nausea, sleeplessness, headaches, and sexual problems, although the newer drugs are less likely to have serious side effects. Antidepressants can also trigger or worsen thoughts of suicide in adolescents.

Another type of medication often used to treat BD is atypical antipsychotics. *Atypical* refers to the fact that these drugs are distinct from older, or conventional, antipsychotics. Antipsychotics primarily help alleviate psychotic symptoms, but they are also effective in quickly controlling severe mania, depression, or mixed episodes.

Commonly used antipsychotics include olanzapine (Zyprexa), aripiprazole (Abilify), quetiapine (Seroquel), and risperidone (Risperdal). All can cause weight gain, diabetes, heart disease, drowsiness, dizziness, blurred vision, skin rashes, and menstrual problems. Some side effects diminish over time, but some do not. Long-term use of antipsychotics can also lead to uncontrollable twitching known as tardive dyskinesia, which many patients find unbearable.

A newer combination pill known as Symbyax contains Zyprexa and Prozac. It appears to treat bipolar depression better than Zyprexa alone does, and some doctors are now prescribing Symbyax along with a mood stabilizer.

Many patients also need medications to help them sleep, and some need antianxiety drugs; however, such medications are not part of standard BD therapy.

Concerns with Drug Therapy

Besides the side effects that can make patients reluctant to take BD drugs, other safety issues exist. Not all BD medications approved for adults are also approved for use in children and adolescents, since side effects, safety, and effectiveness in young people may differ from those in adults. No BD drugs are approved for children under age ten. Several atypical antipsychotics are approved for children aged ten to seventeen, and lithium is approved for ages twelve to seventeen. Doctors often prescribe these and other BD drugs for younger patients for whom they are not approved; this is known as "off-label" use.

Another concern is that no BD medications are approved for use by pregnant women because they place a fetus at high risk for birth defects; however, many pregnant bipolar women choose to continue taking their prescribed medicines because they believe the risks of uncontrolled episodes pose even greater hazards. Some doctors refuse to prescribe these drugs to pregnant women.

The fact that most BD drugs given to outpatients for ongoing treatment take awhile to start working is another issue of concern to many patients. Some drugs take days or even weeks

Although medications are commonly prescribed, some studies indicate that they may pose dangerous medical risks and worsen a BD patient's long-term prognosis.

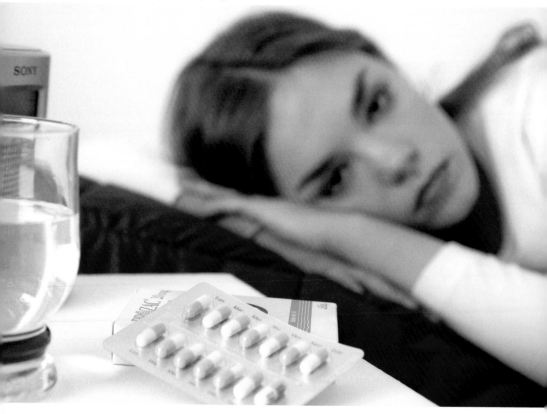

to show results, and many people become impatient and stop taking them. Experts say this is not a good idea. "A person should never stop taking a medication without asking a doctor for help,"[29] states the NIMH.

Studies show that about 50 percent of BD patients stop taking their prescribed medications at some point for various reasons. Men, young people, and those who abuse drugs and alcohol are most likely to stop treatment. Research indicates that people who stop their medications and then start them again during a severe episode are less likely to respond as well as they did the first time around.

A final concern about BD drugs is that several studies indicate that these medications worsen the long-term outlook for patients. A 2007 study at Harvard University, for example, reported that "prognosis for [BD] was once considered relatively favorable, but contemporary findings suggest that disability and poor outcomes are prevalent, despite major therapeutic advances."[30] In the late nineteenth century Emil Kraepelin characterized the long-term outlook for BD patients as good, noting that many people recovered well from episodes and could continue working and living relatively normal lives. Indeed, before the use of BD medications like mood stabilizers became popular, about 85 percent of patients returned to work after episodes. Today, only about 30 percent are able to continue in their occupations, and about 20 percent maintain stable relationships. The unemployment rate among people with BD was about 15 percent in the 1970s and has been 57 to 65 percent since 2000.

The Harvard researchers believe BD drugs may be causing long-term brain damage that impairs patients' ability to think, remember things, and function well. Other experts, however, point out that many people with BD also abuse illegal drugs and alcohol, and that these substances, rather than the bipolar medications, are causing the brain damage. Still other researchers have argued that BD medications reverse, rather than cause, brain damage. A 2009 study at the University of São Paulo in Brazil, for instance, found that long-term lithium use leads to new neuron growth and reverses some of the brain abnormalities that cause BD. The issue of whether the long-term effects of BD drugs are positive or negative has yet to be resolved.

Because of safety concerns, side effects, or ineffectiveness of conventional drug therapy, some patients try alternative therapies such as herbal or other "natural" products. Doctors say some of these products may be harmless, but others are dangerous, and none has proved to be effective. Saint-John's-wort, for example, is an herb widely touted as a natural remedy for depression, but it can cause bipolar patients to cycle from depression to mania and can also lead to headaches and high blood pressure. Experts advise patients to speak with a doctor before trying any alternative product or treatment method. Such treatments are not regulated by the Food and Drug Administration (FDA), and manufacturers and alternative practitioners often make unfounded and exaggerated claims. According to *The Bipolar Disorder Survival Guide*, "There is no evidence that any natural substance is both free of side effects and effective as a mood stabilizer or antidepressant."[31]

Psychotherapy

Whichever medications prove to be best for a particular patient, research shows that combining psychotherapy with drug therapy is more effective than either alone. Psychotherapy usually combines talk therapy with behavior modification. It can be administered by a psychiatrist, psychologist (professional with a PhD in clinical psychology who is licensed to provide psychotherapy, but not to prescribe drugs), social worker, counselor, or psychiatric nurse.

One common type of psychotherapy is cognitive behavior therapy. This helps patients change negative thought and behavior patterns by recognizing how viewing themselves in a negative light leads to harmful emotions and behaviors. As bipolar patient Denise Krischke writes, "When the medications allowed me to achieve some sort of balance, a therapist helped to reshape negative thoughts and behaviors, experienced and

Psychotherapy and counseling for drug or alcohol abuse is usually combined with medications as part of a BD patient's treatment plan.

unintentionally developed into habits during the darkest times. Life takes on a whole new perspective once the chemical monsters are fought. One then has to deal with the internal struggle of having a mental illness and the public's perception of the disorder while attempting to become well."[32]

Another method called psychoeducation teaches patients and their families about every aspect of BD so they can better manage the disorder and recognize impending signs of relapse. A widely used program called the Bipolar Care Model combines psychoeducation administered by nurses with drug treatment prescribed by psychiatrists. It has been found to be especially effective in helping patients take an active role in managing their illness.

Family-focused therapy, like psychoeducation, involves family members and patients and focuses on helping the family develop coping strategies and action plans for dealing with episodes. A similar form of psychotherapy called interpersonal and social rhythm therapy focuses more on the patient himself and helps him learn to improve relationships with others and to establish a regular sleep schedule to protect against episodes.

BD patients with co-occurring substance abuse problems may also need inpatient or outpatient counseling or rehabilitation to treat the substance abuse. Some patients benefit from groups such as Alcoholics Anonymous or from group therapy in a clinic. According to the Depression and Bipolar Support Alliance (DBSA), not treating substance abuse significantly reduces the effectiveness of any BD treatment. The DBSA also recommends that patients be careful about which substance abuse treatment program they choose, since some encourage people to stop taking all drugs, even prescribed ones:

> Some drug and alcohol recovery groups may believe that you can't be clean and sober if you take medications prescribed by a doctor. This belief is just plain wrong. Medication for your mood disorder is no different than medication for another illness such as asthma, high blood pressure or diabetes. If your recovery group challenges your use of medication, it is probably best for you to become part of another group that understands the concept of dual diagnosis.[33]

Electroconvulsive Therapy

In cases where medication and psychotherapy are ineffective, a patient may be given electroconvulsive therapy (ECT). Here, a psychiatrist gives the patient a muscle relaxant and general anesthesia. Then, an electric shock lasting thirty to ninety seconds is administered to the head through electrodes attached

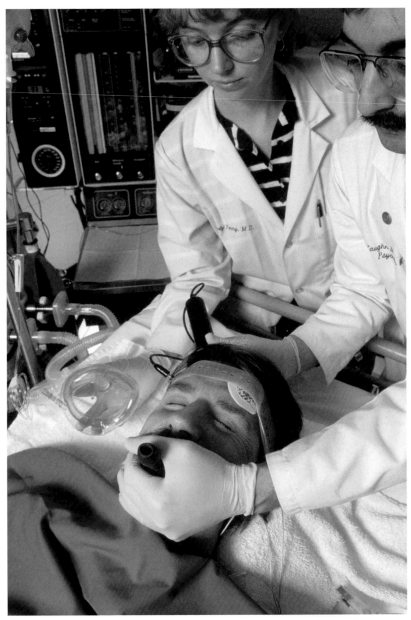

Doctors prepare a patient to receive electroconvulsive therapy, in which a shock is administered to the head. Over time, this procedure is thought to change a person's brain chemistry, and it is sometimes used on BD patients when other therapies have been ineffective.

to the scalp. This produces a seizure that lasts about a minute. Most patients recover within fifteen minutes. ECT is usually given three times per week for two to four weeks. Some patients require ongoing ECT, while others need only occasional follow-up treatments. Doctors believe ECT works by changing brain chemistry.

ECT has been controversial because movies and books like *One Flew Over the Cuckoo's Nest* and many patients' testimonials have depicted it as abusive. Doctors say that while it is true that older forms of ECT were extremely unpleasant for patients and had serious side effects, modern technology has made ECT a tolerable, safe, and fast-acting treatment for those for whom other treatments are ineffective. According to the Mayo Clinic, "Much of the stigma attached to electroconvulsive therapy is based on early treatments in which high doses of electricity were administered without anesthesia, leading to memory loss, fractured bones and other serious side effects. Electroconvulsive therapy is much safer today. . . . It now uses electrical currents given in a controlled setting to achieve the most benefit with the fewest possible risks."[34]

Modern ECT may still cause confusion, slight memory loss, nausea, headache, muscle spasms, and increased blood pressure, but these effects usually go away quickly. Many patients, such as actress Carrie Fisher (known mainly for her role as Princess Leia in the *Star Wars* films), credit ECT with helping them emerge from severe bipolar episodes for which nothing else was effective. Experts point out that ECT is also safer for pregnant women than BD medications are.

Treatment Challenges

Although bipolar treatments are often effective, NAMI points out that about half of the people with BD do not receive any treatment at all, often with devastating results:

> The greatest risk in bipolar disorder is not getting treatment or refusing treatment because of lack of insight into, or inability to resist, the lure of mania. Untreated

people not only experience more frequent or more severe episodes but also suffer higher death rates from medical conditions such as cancer, heart disease, and stroke. One's career, marriage, friendships, and financial stability can be compromised or lost in the face of repeated bouts of depression, recklessness, irrational behavior, drinking or drugging.[35]

Doctors emphasize that starting and sticking with a treatment plan are important; indeed, accepting the need for treatment is one of the primary factors that allows many patients to live fulfilling lives with the disease.

CHAPTER FOUR

Living with Bipolar Disorder

Living with bipolar disorder (BD) is challenging for patients and families, but many people develop methods of coping and living well with the illness, particularly with help from caring medical professionals and strong family support. Living with any chronic disease can be overwhelming, especially at first, and many patients and families experience grief similar to that which occurs when a loved one dies. This is because in a sense, their past quality of life is lost and a new, changed life must begin.

For some, receiving a diagnosis and getting treatment is a reassuring, positive step. Denise Krischke, for example, writes that after experiencing undiagnosed symptoms since childhood, her diagnosis at age twenty-eight "was a blessing to me and my husband because we finally had a name for the out of control behaviors that had overtaken me."[36]

For others, the process of receiving a diagnosis and treatment or even seeking the help that leads to these interventions is filled with anger or denial that anything is wrong. The seductiveness of mania plus other factors unique to BD can make this process especially difficult. Indeed, distinguishing whether certain behaviors stem from a disease or simply reflect a very moody, selfish person can be challenging. "How do you know what is really your illness and what is your 'self' or your personality (your habits, attitudes, and styles of relating to others)?"[37] writes David Miklowitz in *The Bipolar Disorder Survival Guide.*

Family members too may wonder whether to blame an illness or an individual for hurtful, angry behaviors, and many struggle with deciding whether to end the relationship with an unpleasant person. When a person with BD denies that she is ill and refuses to seek help, this can push a spouse or partner to decide not to stay.

Stigma

Another aspect of BD that makes accepting and coping with the disease difficult is the stigma of mental illness. At one time, families hid mentally ill people at home or in institutions out of shame, and seeking help was considered embarrassing at the least. Today, mental illnesses are talked about and tolerated somewhat more, in large part because scientists have discovered biological causes that make others more willing to view these conditions as diseases rather than as weaknesses of character. But stigma still exists and often leads to preconceived notions about "crazy" people and even to overt discrimination.

Many people still view someone with BD or any other mental illness as de facto violent, angry, and dangerous. While this is true of some patients, it is not true of many others. In an article in *BP Magazine*, psychiatrist Ronald Remick of St. Paul's Hospital in Vancouver, British Columbia, Canada, explains, "Bipolar patients are not angry, hostile, irritable people with short fuses. If people with bipolar illness have anger issues, they [merely] have anger issues."[38]

Preconceived ideas can result in others avoiding or refusing to hire or rent a house to a person with BD. Friends may suddenly disappear, and although discrimination in housing or employment is illegal, it happens nonetheless. Oftentimes employers claim that BD makes an individual incapable of performing her job. This is sometimes true, but it is sometimes an excuse for firing someone. Many patients avoid seeking

Because of the stigma of mental illness, some children find it difficult to maintain friendships.

treatment or telling others about their illness for these reasons, hoping that if they pretend nothing is wrong, no one will guess the truth. But often absences due to serious episodes or telltale behaviors give away the secret.

One patient writes that when she returned to her teaching job after a leave of absence, her employer forced her to sign an agreement stating that she would not reveal anything about her bipolar illness to her coworkers or students. This upset her because she knew this would not have happened if she had been hospitalized for an illness such as heart disease.

Stigma can be especially hard on children and families. A child may not understand why others reject him, and the family may be ostracized as well. One mother writes,

> The stigma of bipolar disorder not only affects the person with the illness; it pulls the family members into a painful circle of shame. No matter how much I tell my nine-year-

old daughter who has bipolar disorder that she does not have to be ashamed of her illness, our family still seems to become more and more isolated. Every time she makes a new friend, my mind begins to do a count-down to the end of the friendship.[39]

Once the girl has an episode of screaming rage or something similar, her friend and the friend's parents become frightened, and that is the end of the friendship. Other family members also lose friends who witness the bipolar girl's behavior. The girl's

The Impact of Stigma

In discussing the impact of stigma on people with bipolar disorder, a patient named Denise Krischke writes,

Bipolar disorder is a physical illness with dire emotional and behavioral ramifications. Currently, it is still not perceived as a real illness by many. People see you acting differently from the way you used to act and assume that you are doing it on purpose. . . . I call mental illness a hidden disability both as it is not seen in the person and as the mentally disabled are perceived in society. If we could snap out of it ourselves we would, believe me. No one wants to suffer as we do. I often wished that I could have some physical manifestations of the illness beyond my behavioral and emotional symptoms. A person with a broken arm gets sympathy. A person with a broken brain is the subject of ridicule. We are the brunt of jokes and stigmatizing labels like "crazy," "loony toons," etc. We are ostracized because people do not understand the severity of the distress suffered by one with bipolar disorder.

Denise Krischke. "Bipolar Disorder and Me." Depression and Bipolar Support Alliance. www.dbsalliance.org/site/News2?page=NewsArticle&id=8237&news_iv_ctrl=1042.

mother understands why people do not want to be around an angry or violent child, but at the same time she aches from the isolation that has resulted.

Combating Stigma

Advocacy groups such as the National Alliance on Mental Illness (NAMI) and the Depression and Bipolar Support Alliance (DBSA), along with affected individuals, strive to diminish the stigma of BD by educating the public about the disease and pointing out that people with BD are a diverse and dissimilar group. These advocates also hope that less stigma will lead to

The cast of *Next to Normal,* a stage play about a woman with BD, performs a scene on the 2009 Tony Awards broadcast.

more patients being willing to seek and stick with treatment. One vocal advocate is actress Carrie Fisher. Fisher publicly discusses her battle with BD, often using humor to educate people. She has written a book called *Wishful Drinking* and performs in a one-woman comedy show of the same name. In an interview in *Bipolar Magazine*, Fisher says, "Bipolar disorder is a mood system that functions like the weather. It's independent of the things that happen in your life. I have problems, but they don't have me! . . . I get awards all the time for being mentally ill—I'm a shoo-in because there's no swimsuit competition."[40]

Advocacy groups and individuals have also made headway in encouraging the media to accurately portray people with BD to cut down on stereotypes and misconceptions. In 2009, for example, the Broadway musical *Next to Normal*, which depicted a bipolar woman, won rave reviews and three Tony Awards. Composer Tom Kitt states in a *BP Magazine* interview that audiences responded well because he and lyricist Brian Yorkey strove for accuracy and audience relatability. They spoke with many bipolar patients, as well as with psychiatrists and psychologists, while researching the play. "We both have had experience with bipolar in our own lives and we saw that creating a musical about bipolar was a new way to pull the audience in. We feel the show is filled with empathy and a mixture of sadness, hope, and reality,"[41] he says.

In 2008 the TV hit *Law and Order SVU* aired an episode where Detective Elliot Stabler's teenage daughter is diagnosed with BD, and the show revealed that Stabler's mother also had the disease. Again, the realistic portrayal resonated with viewers and advocates, and the producers reported that they received a great deal of positive feedback. Other television shows such as *ER* and *NYPD Blue* have also aired episodes with a bipolar theme that BD advocates have applauded.

Everyday Challenges

One thing that advocacy and accurate portrayals of BD have brought to light is that living with the disease is a day-to-day struggle that is often beyond the patient's control. A patient named Kyle Rausch aptly sums up this fact when he writes, "I strongly believe that anyone with this disorder never truly owns anything in his or her life. Your loved ones are always one terrible action from being lost; your finances are always one spending binge from being spent; and your life or body are always one risky action from being destroyed or otherwise permanently damaged."[42]

Although medication and other treatments help many patients reduce and control some of these consequences, they are not always effective, and many patients will not stick with a treatment plan. This can result in ongoing risky, abusive, and illegal behaviors. Experts say that while many spouses and other family members try to support and help the person with BD, many times divorce or other drastic actions are necessary for self-protection. When a bipolar patient cannot work, this can lead to further financial and family problems. Bipolar parents also may be unable to care for their children during episodes, and dealing with bipolar children can tear apart families.

Diane, whose ten-year-old bipolar daughter was physically and verbally abusive even with medication, writes, "As a mother, I personally know what it's like to have your life turned upside down. . . . I was afraid one of us would kill the other."[43] Some parents must institutionalize a bipolar child to keep the family safe, and parents find this especially difficult. In other situations, families say that petitioning a court to force treatment or having a bipolar person arrested for illegal activities is one of the most difficult aspects of living with the disease.

Sometimes confronting the patient with an ultimatum is effective in preventing long-term hospitalization or jail. After her bipolar husband drove recklessly with their young daughter in the car, a frustrated wife told him she would tell law enforcement and divorce him if he ever drove anywhere with the girl again. He made an effort to stay on his medications and complied with his wife's ultimatum. But many patients who cannot control their behavior even with medication experience less positive outcomes. One man whose wife divorced him because

A BD patient's inability to stick to a treatment plan and control behavior can result in risky or illegal activities that lead to arrest, sometimes at the request of frustrated family members.

of his abusive and destructive behavior later wrote to apologize to his children, stating, "I did not plan for my episodes to disrupt our lives or frighten the family. Sometimes it's impossible to control them when they overwhelm me and I become a prisoner to my irrational behavior."[44]

Lack of Control

Many people with BD say this lack of control, along with the feeling that others are judging and making decisions about them, is frustrating and demoralizing. In her well-known 1995 book *An Unquiet Mind*, for example, bipolar patient Kay Jamison writes about many such incidents that made her feel less-than-human. One particularly upsetting situation occurred when Jamison's doctor asked her whether she planned to have children. She recalls:

> I told him that I very much wanted to have children, which immediately led to his asking me what I planned to do about taking lithium during pregnancy. I started to tell him that it seemed obvious to me that the dangers of my illness far outweighed any potential problems that lithium might cause a developing fetus, and that I therefore would choose to stay on my lithium. Before I finished, however, he broke in to ask me if I knew that manic-depressive illness was a genetic disease. . . . I wasn't entirely stupid, I said, "Yes, of course." At that point, in an icy and imperious voice that I can hear to this day, he stated . . . "You shouldn't have children." I felt sick, unbelievably and utterly sick, and deeply humiliated. I asked him if his concerns about my having children stemmed from the fact that, because of my illness, I would be an inadequate mother or simply that he thought it was best to avoid bringing another manic-depressive into the world. Ignoring or missing my sarcasm, he replied, "Both."[45]

Many patients change doctors or refuse to accept treatment because they feel dehumanized by the physician's attitude. But most doctors make every effort to treat their patients with respect, since this is one factor that increases the chances that the person will view his treatment program as a partnership with the doctor and will stick with the therapy.

Living Well with Bipolar Disorder

Besides forging an ongoing partnership with a physician to manage BD, experts and patients find that several other adjustments and attitudes are important for living as well as possible with the illness. Doctors say patients who accept the fact that they have a chronic disease and that they must make changes in their lives to control it have the best quality of life. By accepting the disease, experts say, patients take some control of BD rather than allowing it to completely control them.

Some patients with BD find that tai chi, yoga, and other relaxation techniques are helpful in managing the disease.

A teen named Michelle, for instance, refused to accept her condition or to take her prescribed medications for several years after her diagnosis at age twelve. She was hospitalized repeatedly, and finally realized that she would be better off if she changed her attitude and stuck with a treatment plan. Her life improved dramatically, and she even started seeing some positive aspects of having a serious illness. As she writes, "I learned life lessons at a young age that I will know forever. Some people don't learn these lessons until they're much older. Some people never learn them. One of my closest friends also has bipolar disorder. He always tells me to think of it as a gift and not something bad because it helps you look at life in different ways. With this illness you see things you never would have otherwise."[46]

In addition to accepting and treating BD, doctors recommend that patients also take steps to live a healthier lifestyle overall. Practicing relaxation techniques such as yoga or tai chi, getting regular exercise, and eating a well-balanced diet not only improve physical health, but also help people cope by promoting positive changes in brain chemistry. Doctors say that avoiding excessive amounts of sugar, caffeine, and alcohol are especially important in helping regulate mood. People with BD who work in jobs that require irregular hours and a lot of travel also do better if they switch to positions with consistent hours that allow them to keep a regular sleep schedule.

Social Support

Having adequate family and social support can also help patients cope and live fully, and experts advise ending or improving stressful relationships and not associating with people who are a negative influence. At the same time, encouraging family members and friends to educate themselves about BD and to actively participate in an ongoing action plan so they can reinforce the patient's efforts to maintain control is another positive step. Many patients find that they learn who their true friends are when these individuals are willing to help out. Family members are especially important in helping patients recover and stay stable.

How to Help a Loved One Who Has Bipolar Disorder

The Depression and Bipolar Support Alliance (DBSA) offers the following advice to BD patients' family members and friends who wish to be helpful:

What you can say that helps:
- You are not alone in this. I'm here for you.
- I understand you have a real illness and that's what causes these thoughts and feelings.
- You may not believe it now, but the way you're feeling will change.
- I may not be able to understand exactly how you feel, but I care about you and want to help.
- When you want to give up, tell yourself you will hold on for just one more day, hour, minute—whatever you can manage.
- You are important to me. Your life is important to me.
- Tell me what I can do now to help you.
- I am here for you.
- We will get through this together.

What you should avoid saying:
- It's all in your head.
- We all go through times like this.
- You'll be fine. Stop worrying.
- Look on the bright side.
- You have so much to live for, why do you want to die?
- I can't do anything about your situation.
- Just snap out of it.
- Stop acting crazy.
- What's wrong with you?
- Shouldn't you be better by now?

Depression and Bipolar Support Alliance. "Helping Someone with a Mood Disorder." www.dbsalliance.org/site/PageServer?pagename=about_helping.

When the patient and family sit down to discuss past episodes and pinpoint early signs that can reveal an impending episode, they are able to develop a plan to notify the patient's physician and take other steps to prevent the episode from spiraling out of control. Family members learn to look for common early signs of mania that may include sleep disturbances, making ambitious plans, talking nonstop, or becoming confrontational. Signs of impending depression can be less obvious, but may include negative thoughts, sadness, tiredness, withdrawing from social situations, and having trouble sleeping and concentrating.

Support from family and friends is a critical aspect of managing BD for most patients. Loved ones can keep an eye out for specific behaviors or triggers and help a patient stick to a treatment plan.

For some patients, having a family member help with keeping track of events that consistently precede an episode can also help with prevention. These events may include a suddenly hectic schedule at work, an important test at school, partying with friends, or a confrontation with a spouse or partner. Once the patient and family member document the triggering events, a therapist can then help the patient develop methods of avoiding such situations. Taking a few days off work, not leaving all the studying for a test until the last minute, or telling friends that it is impossible to go out drinking with them anymore are all possible methods of avoiding these situations.

Many people with BD and their families also draw up written contracts that give certain family members permission to take steps to rein in the patient's behavior if the lure of mania makes her unable to see that she is about to do regrettable things. The family member can take away the patient's credit cards and checkbook, take the person to the psychiatrist even if he does not want to go, or forbid him to make important decisions such as changing jobs, getting married or divorced, or moving. Although a pre-manic person may not see the need for such restrictions, many find that previously signing a contract prevents unfortunate consequences time after time.

Support Groups and Advocacy

Many patients and families find that participating in local or online support groups is also invaluable for recognizing early signs of episodes and for coping in general. Support groups consist of individuals dealing with the same illness and its problems. Some are led by a facilitator, while others meet more informally to share information and compassion. Because group members have "been there, done that," they are often very helpful in alerting people about impending episodes and offering coping strategies. One DBSA study found that participation in a support group improved patients' treatment compliance by about 94 percent as well.

Support groups can also assist people with making important decisions. Paul, whose wife has BD, was thinking of leaving her because of her promiscuous behavior during manic episodes. The couple began attending a local support group, and Paul found it extremely helpful in motivating him to give his wife another chance. "The people in the group were great," he says. "They all had stories like ours—some a whole lot worse, it was amazing—and they all poured out sympathy. It was like being with a bunch of war veterans—we bonded pretty quickly over our bad experiences, and I got a lot of really good advice. It also helped to see other people struggling to keep their marriages together and succeeding."[47]

Many people find that reaching out to help others through support groups, advocacy organizations, or other avenues also improves their own lives. Andy Behrman, for example, wrote *Electroboy: A Memory of Mania* to help others by sharing his experiences and found he developed a sense of pride from serving as a source of hope. "I thought that my sharing my story—a very personal story—would bring people out of the closet to seek treatment, help family members in understanding their loved ones, and also help mental healthcare professionals in treating their patients. . . . Passing on my knowledge of my coping skills is the most important thing that I can do with my life,"[48] he writes.

Before achieving stability, Behrman endured being misdiagnosed for ten years, trying nearly forty different medications, undergoing ECT, losing his job as a public relations agent and art dealer, and going to jail for counterfeiting art while in a manic state. Many patients garner hope from his story and from the stories of others who live successfully with BD.

The fact that many famous, creative, successful people battle and have battled the disease is also a source of hope for many. Composers Ludwig van Beethoven, Pyotr Tchaikovsky, and Georg Friedrich Handel; artist Vincent van Gogh; actresses Marilyn Monroe, Vivian Leigh, Margot Kidder, Carrie Fisher, and Patty Duke; writers Edgar Allan Poe and Mark Twain; talk show host Dick Cavett; and British prime minister Winston Churchill

BD patients and their families can benefit from participating in support groups to share experiences and coping strategies.

are among the celebrities known or suspected of having or having had BD. In fact, many experts have stated that while severe BD has devastating effects, mild hypomania is often associated with creativity, the drive to pursue unconventional and innovative goals, and optimism that leads to a strong work ethic and productivity.

Success stories, however, are balanced by many patients whose lives are ongoing nightmares or who take their own lives because of despair. Experts and affected people agree that there is still much to do in the future before the personal and societal impact of bipolar disorder can be diminished.

CHAPTER FIVE

The Future and Bipolar Disorder

The personal and societal impact of bipolar disorder (BD) has led medical experts, health advocates, and government officials to call for increased education and research to try to diminish the suffering and social effects of the disorder in the future. Not only does BD cost individuals, insurance companies, and the government billions of dollars each year, but people with the illness also develop other serious diseases such as heart disease, stroke, cancer, and diabetes more often than the general public does. This results in additional health care costs and suffering.

The Most Expensive Mental Disorder

According to the National Alliance on Mental Illness (NAMI), "Bipolar disorder is the most expensive mental health care diagnosis, both for patients with the illness and for their health insurance plans."[49] The Centers for Disease Control and Prevention (CDC) attributes this primarily to direct medical costs for hospitalizations and ongoing treatment, as well as to indirect costs from patients' not being stable enough to work. Since hospitalizations are far costlier than outpatient treatment, insurance companies, along with doctors and the government (which pays for medical costs for poor or disabled people) are attempting to educate patients about the importance of staying with an outpatient treatment plan.

Medical experts estimate BD costs individuals and society in the United States over $50 billion each year in direct health care costs alone, and much more in indirect costs, such as paying for unemployment benefits and for expenses incurred in the criminal justice system by patients who break the law while manic. Ongoing studies are assessing methods of diminishing

The ability to maintain employment allows a BD patient to build self-esteem, social interactions, and economic independence. The National Institute of Mental Health has created programs to support those with BD in developing the skills needed to get and keep jobs.

Improving Patient Access to Treatment

Because many people with bipolar disorder (BD) do not receive treatment, a current National Institute of Mental Health (NIMH) study is evaluating how to best improve patient access to the newest and best treatments. Researchers are studying whether a program called the Bipolar Care Model can be "packaged" and efficiently delivered to patients in community mental health clinics, which are generally more accessible to patients than hospitals and private doctors are. The investigators are making Bipolar Care Model manuals available to selected clinics and offering training and technical assistance to health care professionals at these clinics. Later on, they plan to evaluate whether or not people working at the clinics followed the model and whether patients' symptoms and quality of life improved after six, twelve, and twenty-four months.

The Bipolar Care Model combines personalized drug treatment prescribed by a psychiatrist with psychoeducation administered by psychiatric nurses. These nurses help patients learn about BD, recognize the signs of an impending relapse, and develop an action plan for preventing episodes from getting out of control. Studies have shown that the model greatly improves treatment success and patients' quality of life while also lowering the cost of bipolar care.

the economic and social impact of these costs, as well as looking for ways of helping people with BD to improve the quality of their lives.

One such study being conducted by the National Institute of Mental Health (NIMH) is comparing the effectiveness of two supportive programs in helping people with severe mental illness find and keep jobs. Many bipolar people have trouble getting and keeping a job because their mental instability and problems with attention and inability to problem solve can prevent them from being reliable workers. Thus, the NIMH study is evaluating methods of improving attention, problem solving, and other mental processes that can help patients become more dependable and hard working. Previous studies have found that unemployed people who manage to obtain and keep a job experience enhanced self-esteem and improved social skills and economic status. This is good not only for the individual and his family, but also for society in general.

The first program in the NIMH study is called IPS-CT (Individual Placement and Support Plus Cognitive Training). It helps place and support patients in jobs in their communities and offers vocational counseling that helps these individuals recognize and change the negative thought patterns that set them up for failure when they look for and land a job. The program also teaches methods of improving attention, memory, and problem-solving abilities.

The second program, IPS-ES (Individual Placement and Support Plus Enhanced Support), adds more-frequent and more-detailed vocational counseling to the IPS-CT model. During the study, doctors and counselors are comparing psychiatric symptoms, job satisfaction, quality of life, and thinking, learning, memory, and problem-solving skills in patients in both groups at regular intervals.

Addressing Prevalence and Prevention

Since the increasing number of people diagnosed with BD has fueled the vast economic burden and forced more and more families to deal with the disorder, several research projects seek to diminish associated costs and suffering by clarifying and improving diagnostic criteria so fewer people will be misdiagnosed and more will receive appropriate treatment. In one NIMH study, scientists led by Dr. Ellen Leibenluft are addressing recent evidence showing that many doctors are overdiagnosing BD in children and adolescents who actually have other disorders such as attention deficit/hyperactivity disorder. The researchers are carefully documenting the mood and behavior patterns seen in children with BD and other disorders and are also using magnetic resonance imaging (MRI) and functional magnetic resonance imaging (fMRI) to study how the brains of children with these various diseases differ. They hope that someday these imaging techniques can be used to objectively distinguish and diagnose these disorders.

Leibenluft and her colleagues have also proposed adding new disorders to the *Diagnostic and Statistical Manual* to give doctors more opportunities to correctly diagnose conditions that resemble but differ from BD. They have suggested that new disorders called severe mood dysregulation (SMD) and temper dysregulation with dysphoria (TDD) should be diagnosed in children who seem to have BD but do not satisfy all the criteria and do not go on to develop adult BD. SMD and TDD both involve aggression, irritability, temper tantrums, and unhappiness, but the symptoms are ongoing rather than occurring in discrete episodes like adult BD does. At the present time doctors usually diagnose such children with BD, since the current diagnostic criteria allow symptoms in children and teens to vary somewhat from those in adults.

In related research, investigators are exploring methods of preventing full-blown BD in at-risk children. Doctors consider these efforts to be especially important in light of the dramatic increases in childhood cases of the disease. One NIMH study is assessing whether family-based therapy and psychoeducation delay or prevent a first manic, hypomanic, or depressive episode in at-risk children and teens. Researchers determine at-risk status by evaluating the family history and the child's history of mood and behavior problems. Children deemed to be at-risk for BD must have one or both parents or a sibling diagnosed with BD and must be previously diagnosed with cyclothymia, depression, or bipolar disorder not otherwise specified.

Since the family environment plays a role in determining whether or not an at-risk child develops full-blown BD, the experimental therapy in this study attempts to improve this environment by educating the family about mood disorders and teaching them how to effectively communicate and cope with a child's moodiness or behavior problems.

Researchers have developed programs to better recognize and diagnose BD in children and adolescents, including the ability to distinguish it from conditions with similar symptoms.

Another NIMH study is testing the effectiveness of a type of therapy called behavioral interpersonal psychotherapy in preventing full-blown BD or allowing early detection of BD in teens who have a parent with the disease. The researchers hope that this therapy, which focuses on changing disruptive behaviors and family interactions, can "override" a genetic predisposition to the illness. According to the NIMH,

> Research suggests that children of parents with BD are at risk for developing mood disorders because of predisposing genetic factors and stressful life events, many of which may be related to their parents' unstable clinical state. Adolescent children of parents with BD must deal simultaneously

with the difficult task of negotiating their own developmental transitions, as well as living with a parent with BD. It may be possible to detect symptoms of BD or other mood disorders early in adolescence and prevent the disorder from further interfering with someone's life.[50]

Research on Causes

Hand-in-hand with research on improving diagnosis and prevention, many scientists are attempting to better understand the causes of BD in hopes of improving treatments and quality of life for patients. Some studies are searching for more gene mutations that are linked to BD. Researchers believe that finding a complete set of genes that contribute to a genetic predisposition can then lead to a better understanding of how the chemicals produced as a result of instructions from these genes interact to increase susceptibility.

Related studies are evaluating how different neurotransmitters contribute to BD. Previous research has documented how serotonin, norepinephrine, glutamate, GABA (gamma-aminobutyric acid), and several other neurotransmitters play a role, and new NIMH research is using fMRI to see how the neurotransmitter acetylcholine affects behavior and thought patterns in people with the illness. Acetylcholine is known to affect memory and attention, and scientists believe that areas in the brain that produce and respond to acetylcholine may become overly sensitive during depressive episodes. The researchers are evaluating how the drug scopolamine, which diminishes acetylcholine activity, affects memory and attention when patients are depressed.

Other studies at several medical centers are using MRI to assess differences in the brains of people with BD, those with a genetic predisposition to BD but no signs of illness, and healthy control subjects. Brain imaging is also being used to assess how BD medications correct the brain abnormalities seen in patients. One NIMH-sponsored study is using fMRI to determine whether lithium changes activity and blood flow in various areas of the brain. Patients in the study undergo fMRI while researchers present pictures, letters, words, and sounds that elicit an emotional response, both before and after treatment with lithium. Scientists believe lithium acts by correcting abnormal brain activity in several brain areas, but are not yet sure how it achieves this.

Research on Treatment

One goal of furthering an understanding of the brain changes that cause BD is to develop treatments that specifically target these areas. This, in turn, doctors hypothesize, may make these therapies more tolerable than existing treatments are. Researchers are focusing on testing new drugs and nondrug therapies, assessing which drug combinations are most effective, and evaluating the safety of drug treatments for the rapidly expanding population of children with BD.

Investigators test drugs and other therapies in clinical trials by dividing patients into an experimental and a control group. Those in the experimental group receive the treatment being tested, while those in the control group receive a placebo, or a fake that looks like the real thing. This allows scientists to determine whether any improvements are due to the treatment itself rather than to the patient's expectation of success.

One drug being tested is ketamine, which is currently approved as an anesthetic for human and veterinary medicine. Ketamine is also used illegally as a club drug because of its ability to induce hallucinations and a dreamlike state. It works by blocking NMDA (N-methyl-D-aspartate) receptors in the brain. These receptors are part of the glutamate system, which plays a role in depression. A preliminary study on a small number of bipolar patients indicated that ketamine administered by a doctor can be a fast-acting antidepressant in people for whom other treatments have been unsuccessful. According to a Reuters Health article, "The 18 patients in the study had tried an average of seven different drugs for treating their bipolar illness, and were still severely depressed; 55 percent had failed electroconvulsive therapy (ECT), or shock treatment. But within 40 minutes of receiving a ketamine injection, their depressive symptoms improved; the effect persisted for at least three days."[51] Researchers are now experimenting to determine optimal doses and frequency of administration and plan to test the safety and effectiveness of ketamine in studies with larger groups of patients.

Another drug under investigation is currently approved for the treatment of Alzheimer's disease because it slightly improves cognitive abilities and memory. Since people with BD have some similar attention and memory problems, scientists believe this medication, known as galantamine, may be helpful for BD as well. Galantamine raises levels of acetylcholine in the brain.

The drug ketamine, an anesthetic used in humans and animals, has shown promise for BD patients as a treatment for depressive symptoms.

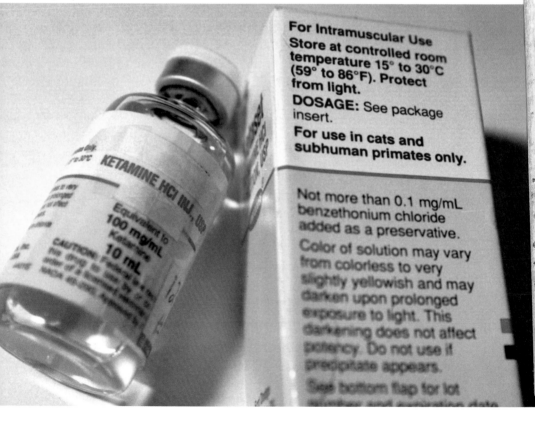

In research on combinations of drugs, scientists are testing various combinations of mood stabilizers, antidepressants, anticonvulsants, and antipsychotics to assess whether combining these medications reduces the incidence of relapses and controls acute episodes more than each drug alone does. Other research on drug combinations is addressing the feasibility of treating both BD and alcoholism at the same time. A study at the University of Cincinnati, for example, is evaluating the effectiveness of combining the antipsychotic quetiapine with the anticonvulsant topiramate for the treatment of co-occurring alcoholism and BD in adolescents and young adults.

Since drugs can have different effects in children and adolescents than they do in adults, additional studies are trying to determine safe and effective doses of BD drugs approved for adults when these medications are given to children. According to the National Institutes of Health Clinical Center, "Pediatric BD is often difficult to treat; children may respond only partially to the medications now available or have too many side effects to tolerate them."[52] One clinical trial is testing riluzole, which reduces the amount of glutamate in the brain, in children with BD. Riluzole has previously been shown to help adults with depression, and it is also used to treat amyotrophic lateral sclerosis (ALS, or Lou Gehrig's disease) in adults. If it proves to be effective in bipolar children, riluzole would be the first antiglutamate drug approved for bipolar depression in children.

Research on Natural Substances

Many patients of all ages would prefer to take natural remedies that have fewer side effects than existing conventional BD drugs do, so scientists are also testing the safety and effectiveness of alternative substances. One natural substance that has been touted as an effective antidepressant is omega-3 fatty acids, which are found in fish, walnuts, and flaxseed and are available in pill form. Many people take omega-3 fatty acids to reduce high cholesterol as well. Doctors at the University of Cincinnati believe these compounds may alleviate depression and prevent manic episodes when given to people with BD, and a current study is evaluating this hypothesis. Previous studies

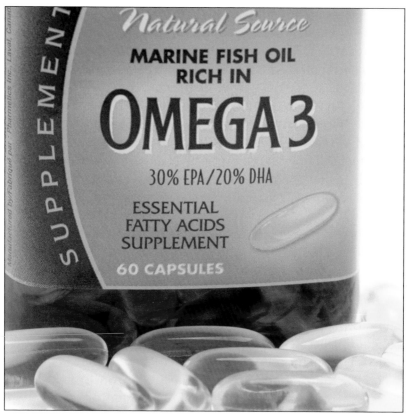

Omega-3 fatty acids, which are found in some foods and in pill form, have been shown in some studies to alleviate depression and prevent manic episodes in people with BD.

have found varying results—one study indicated omega-3s prevented relapses, but another found it to be ineffective. If omega-3s prove to be a viable treatment for BD, they would represent a safe method of attacking the disease.

Another compound being tested is uridine. The human liver produces this substance, and it is involved in many body functions, such as the use of energy by cells. There is some evidence that uridine is effective in treating depression in bipolar adults, and researchers at the University of Utah are now testing it in bipolar adolescents. The investigators are assessing improvements in mood with standardized rating scales and are also using MRI and magnetic resonance spectroscopy (MRS) scans to determine how uridine acts on the brain. Based on previous research, they believe uridine changes levels of the brain chemical beta-nucleoside triphosphate in the anterior cingulate cortex. Beta-nucleoside triphosphate is associated with energy metabolism in the brain, and the investigators hypothesize that correcting abnormal beta-nucleoside triphosphate levels in the brain will correct the deficiencies in energy metabolism that partially underlie BD.

Nondrug Treatments

In addition to new types of drug therapy, researchers are evaluating several nondrug treatments. One experimental treatment

Exercise and Bipolar Disorder

While exercise alone does not effectively treat bipolar disorder (BD), getting regular exercise has been documented as enhancing the positive effects of other treatment elements. It also helps prevent some of the other health problems, such as heart disease, that often affect people with BD. In hopes of motivating more patients to increase their physical activity, a National Institute of Mental Health study is evaluating the effectiveness of a peer support system.

Participants enroll in an exercise program that includes group classes and supervised individual exercise at a gym three times per week. One group of patients also receives peer support for fifteen minutes per week from an educator who provides information about the benefits of exercise and gives pep talks designed to reinforce participation in the program. A control group does the exercises but receives no peer support.

The researchers are measuring and comparing patients' cardiovascular fitness, weight, amount of exercise done each week, depression, reported quality of life, and other indicators of improved health at specified intervals in both groups.

is deep brain stimulation. Here, doctors implant a nerve stimulator into the patient's upper chest and also place electrodes
that receive signals from the stimulator into specific areas of
the brain. The procedure is currently approved for the treatment of Parkinson's disease, and experts believe it may also
be effective for bipolar patients for whom nothing else works.
Brain surgery poses serious risks, such as bleeding, stroke,
breathing and heart problems, seizures, movement disorders,

An X-ray shows electrodes placed in the brain of a patient
undergoing deep brain stimulation, a treatment used on patients
with Parkinson's disease that shows promise for those with BD.

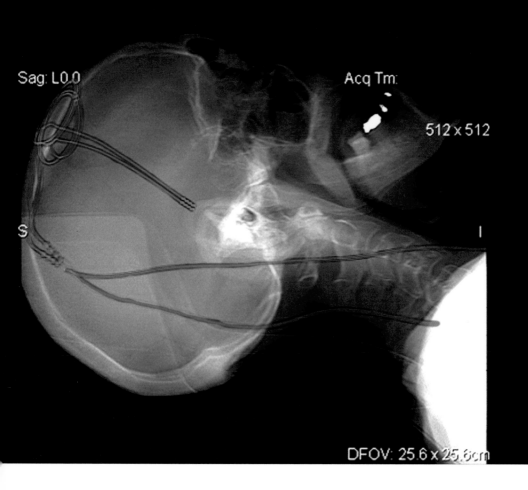

and mood and cognitive changes, so doctors emphasize that should it prove effective for BD, deep brain stimulation would only be used in dire circumstances.

A similar treatment called vagus nerve stimulation is less risky, but still not widely used for any purpose because of its side effects, which can include hoarseness, coughing, and shortness of breath. It is currently approved to treat unipolar depression that does not respond to other treatments and is now being tested in people with BD. With vagus nerve stimulation, doctors insert a small generator attached to wires in the left side of the chest. The wires are connected to the vagus nerve in the neck. The vagus nerve is responsible for relaying signals from the rest of the body to the brain. When the generator in the chest is turned on, electrical pulses are transmitted to areas of the brain associated with depression, and this appears to change the biochemistry in those areas.

Other experimental procedures use magnetic fields rather than electrical currents. One such therapy is magnetic seizure therapy, which is similar to ECT, except it uses a magnetic field to generate a seizure. Like ECT, magnetic seizure therapy is performed when a patient is under general anesthesia. Unlike ECT, which shocks the whole brain, magnetic seizure therapy can be focused on specific areas of the brain. It thus seems to avoid the memory loss often seen with ECT, though patients still show some short-term confusion. If magnetic seizure therapy proves to be effective, doctors hope it will offer bipolar patients who are not helped by medications a new treatment option.

Another experimental therapy that uses magnetic fields, transcranial magnetic stimulation, does not require the use of anesthesia and can be performed in a doctor's office rather than in a hospital. With transcranial magnetic stimulation, a physician places an electromagnetic generator on the patient's scalp, and magnetic pulses are sent to parts of the brain that regulate mood. The treatment lasts for thirty to forty minutes. Experts believe the pulses induce biochemical changes in the brain similar to those that occur during other procedures that use electrical or magnetic stimulation. Tran-scranial magnetic stimulation seems to be safe and effective for treating unipolar depression, and scientists are now testing it in people with BD.

Also effective in treating a variety of unipolar depression is phototherapy, a treatment using light. This treatment often helps people with seasonal affective disorder, which is a type of depression that occurs during the fall and winter months. Doctors have found that the shorter amounts of daylight in winter trigger depression in some individuals.

Light therapy uses a light box or a light visor to deliver bright light to the patient during the time of year when they have symptoms. Sometimes this is administered in a doctor's office, and at other times a patient rents or purchases the device to use at home. The patient sits near the light box, and the light must indirectly enter the eyes in order for the treatment to be effective. The individual cannot, however, look directly at the light or it can harm the eyes. A typical treatment session lasts from thirty minutes to two hours, depending on the particular light box and the patient's needs. Side effects are generally mild, when they even occur, and may include headache, eyestrain, and sleep disturbances.

Since light therapy often helps people with seasonal affective disorder, researchers believe it may also be effective for bipolar patients during the depressive phase of their illness. This belief is based on the fact that the internal biological clock that responds to light in the environment is known to play a role in causing BD. Preliminary studies on several people with bipolar depression indicate that light therapy administered during the middle of the day is often effective in alleviating this depression, but the same treatment in the morning is much less effective and even leads to mixed states in some cases. With seasonal affective disorder, on the other hand, early morning therapy is most effective. Experts are not sure why this is true. A current study at the University of Pittsburgh is testing different durations of light therapy to determine which is most effective in people with bipolar depression.

Patients with BD can benefit from light therapy, a treatment used on people with seasonal affective disorder that may be helpful during depressive episodes.

Outlook for the Future

The goal of all of these research, education, and advocacy efforts is to help more people with bipolar disorder live better lives and see more positive results from their treatment plans. The ultimate goal is a cure for BD that will allow affected people to escape from the ongoing struggles that the disease imposes on them. Although much progress in diagnosis, treatment, and understanding BD has been made over the past several decades, experts say many challenges lie ahead before these goals can be realized. In discussing the outlook for the future of bipolar disorder, a DBSA article states, "There is still much to explore in the body and brain. As research continues, we'll understand more and more about the brain and illnesses like depression and bipolar disorder. As time goes on, maybe this new understanding will help us design a better map for those who feel like they are lost in the struggles of life with a mood disorder. And maybe this map will be one of the tools that helps them find their way on the road to recovery."[53]

Notes

Introduction: Why the Increasing Numbers of Bipolar Disorder?

1. Quoted in Irene M. Wielawski. "Diagnosing Mood Disorders in a New Generation." *New York Times*, January 25, 2008. www.nytimes.com/ref/health/healthguide/esn-bipolar-qa.html.
2. Roger Z. Samuel, M.D. Letter to the editor in response to "Bipolar Disorder in Children and Adolescents—in Session with Kiki Chang, M.D." *Primary Psychiatry*, vol. 17, no. 9, 2010. www.primarypsychiatry.com/aspx/articledetail.aspx?articleid=2823.
3. Samuel. Letter to the editor.
4. Robert J. Hedaya, M.D. "Highest Rates of Bipolar Disorder in the United States: Why?" *Psychology Today*, March 10, 2011. www.psychologytoday.com/blog/health-matters/2011 03/highest-rates-bipolar-disorder-in-the-united-states-why.

Chapter One: What Is Bipolar Disorder?

5. National Institute of Mental Health. "Bipolar Disorder." Washington, DC: U.S. Dept. of Health and Human Services, 2008. www.nimh.nih.gov/health/publications/bipolar-disorder/complete-index.shtml.
6. Aretaeus. *The Extant Works of Aretaeus, the Cappadocian*. Edited and translated by Francis Adams. Boston: Boston Milford House, 1972, p. 299.
7. Linda. "Human Yo-Yo." Depression and Bipolar Support Alliance, March 27, 2006. www.dbsalliance.org/site/News2?page=NewsArticle&id=6048&news_iv_ctrl=1042.
8. National Institute of Mental Health. "Bipolar Disorder."
9. National Alliance on Mental Illness. "Understanding Bipolar Disorder and Recovery." Arlington, VA: NAMI, August 2008. www.nami.org/Template.cfm?Section=By

_Illness&template=/ContentManagement/ContentDisplay .cfm&ContentID=67728.

10. Quoted in David J. Miklowitz. *The Bipolar Disorder Survival Guide*. New York: Guilford, 2011, p. 20.

11. Kaity B. "Holding My Breath." Depression and Bipolar Support Alliance, June 2, 2011. www.dbsalliance.org/site /News2?page=NewsArticle&id=9095&news_iv_ctrl=1042.

12. Aretaeus. *The Extant Works*, pp. 302–303.

13. Medifocus. *Medifocus Guidebook on Bipolar Disorder*. Silver Spring, MD: Medifocus, 2011, pp. 50–51.

14. Chelsea Lowe and Bruce M. Cohen, M.D. *Living with Someone Who's Living with Bipolar Disorder*. San Francisco: Jossey-Bass, 2010, p. 8.

15. Andy Behrman. "My Ten-Year Anniversary." Electroboy, 2005. www.electroboy.com/article13-tenyearanniversary .shtml.

16. Quoted in Depression and Bipolar Support Alliance. "You've Just Been Diagnosed . . . What Now?" www.dbs alliance.org/site/DocServer/FINAL_JustDiagnosed_AYS _AfrAmer.pdf?.docID=2921.

Chapter Two: What Causes Bipolar Disorder?

17. Aretaeus. *The Extant Works*, p. 302.

18. National Institute of Mental Health. "Bipolar Disorder."

19. Quoted in National Institutes of Health. "Major Ups and Downs." *News in Health*, May 2010. http://newsinhealth .nih.gov/issue/May2010/Feature1.

20. C.A. McClung. "Role for the CLOCK Gene in Bipolar Disorder." Association for Applied Psychophysiology and Biofeedback. www.aapb.org/ar/act-cient/23-McClung_S72 .pdf.

21. Lowe and Cohen. *Living with Someone Who's Living with Bipolar Disorder*, p. 34.

22. Quoted in National Institutes of Health. "Major Ups and Downs."

23. Miklowitz. *The Bipolar Disorder Survival Guide*, p. 80.

24. Laurie Nedvin. "The Ultimate Betrayal." Depression and Bipolar Support Alliance, November 13, 2009. www.dbs

alliance.org/site/News2?page=NewsArticle&id=8507&news
_iv_ctrl=1042.

Chapter Three: How Is Bipolar Disorder Treated?

25. Miklowitz. *The Bipolar Disorder Survival Guide*, p. 133.
26. Miklowitz. *The Bipolar Disorder Survival Guide*, p. 7.
27. National Alliance on Mental Illness, "Bipolar Disorder."
    www.nami.org/Template.cfm?Section=By_Illness&Template
    =/TaggedPage/TaggedPageDisplay.cfm&TPLID=54&Content
    ID=23037.
28. Gary S. Sachs et al. "Effectiveness of Adjunctive Antide-
    pressant Treatment for Bipolar Depression." *New Eng-
    land Journal of Medicine*, April 26, 2007. www.nejm.org
    /doi/full/10.1056/NEJMoa064135#t=articleTop.
29. National Institute of Mental Health. "Mental Health Medi-
    cations." www.nimh.nih.gov/health/publications/mental
    -health-medications/complete-index.shtml.
30. Nancy Huxley and Ross J. Baldessarini. "Disability and Its
    Treatment in Bipolar Disorder Patients." *Bipolar Disor-
    ders*, vol. 9, 2007, p. 183.
31. Miklowitz. *The Bipolar Disorder Survival Guide*, p. 107.
32. Denise Krischke. "Bipolar Disorder and Me." Depression
    and Bipolar Support Alliance. www.dbsalliance.org/site
    /News2?page=NewsArticle&id=8237&news_iv_ctrl=1042.
33. Depression and Bipolar Support Alliance. "Dual Diagnosis
    and Recovery," August 2003. www.dbsalliance.org/pdfs
    /dualdiag.pdf.
34. The Mayo Clinic. "Electroconvulsive Therapy (ECT)."
    www.mayoclinic.com/health/electroconvulsive-therapy
    /MY00129.
35. National Alliance on Mental Illness. "Understanding Bipo-
    lar Disorder and Recovery."

Chapter Four: Living with Bipolar Disorder

36. Krischke. "Bipolar Disorder and Me."
37. Miklowitz. *The Bipolar Disorder Survival Guide*, p. 56.
38. Quoted in *Bipolar Magazine*. "Stuck on the Rage Road,"
    Fall 2008. www.nami.org/Template.cfm?Section=Bipolar

_Disorder&template=/ContentManagement/ContentDisplay
.cfm&ContentID=67735.

39. Debra. "Fighting the Circle of Shame." Depression and Bipolar Support Alliance, March 27, 2006. www.dbsalliance
.org/site/News2?page=NewsArticle&id=5998&news_iv_
ctrl=1043.

40. Quoted in Nancy Tobin. "The Wit and Wisdom of Carrie
Fisher." *bphope.com* (blog). www.bphope.com/item.aspx
?id=630.

41. Quoted in Nancy Tobin. "Tackling Stigma from the Stage."
bphope.com (blog). www.bphope.com/item.aspx?id=593.

42. Kyle Rausch. "A Cruel Joke." Depression and Bipolar
Support Alliance, September 22, 2009. www.dbsalliance
.org/site/News2?page=NewsArticle&id=8423&news_iv
_ctrl=1042.

43. Diane. "Caring for a Child with Bipolar1." Depression
and Bipolar Support Alliance, March 27, 2006. www.dbs
alliance.org/site/News2?page=NewsArticle&id=6002&news
_iv_ctrl=1042.

44. Chuck. "Open All Night?" Depression and Bipolar Support
Alliance, March 27, 2006. www.dbsalliance.org/site/News
2?page=NewsArticle&id=5991&news_iv_ctrl=1042.

45. K.R. Jamison. *An Unquiet Mind.* New York: Knopf, 1995,
p. 191.

46. Michelle. "A Teen Trying to Live." Depression and Bipolar
Support Alliance, March 27, 2006. www.dbsalliance.org
/site/News2?page=NewsArticle&id=6068&news_iv_ctrl
=1042.

47. Quoted in Lowe and Cohen. *Living with Someone Who's
Living with Bipolar Disorder*, p. 103.

48. Behrman. "My Ten-Year Anniversary."

Chapter Five: The Future and Bipolar Disorder

49. National Alliance on Mental Illness. "The Impact and Cost
of Mental Illness: The Case of Bipolar Disorder." www.nami
.org/Content/NavigationMenu/Inform_Yourself/About_Pub
lic_Policy/Policy_Research_Institute/Policymakers_Toolkit
/Impact_and_Cost_of_Mental_Illness_the_Case_of_Bipolar
_Disorder.pdf.

50. National Institute of Mental Health. "Early Detection and Prevention of Mood Disorders in Children of Parents with Bipolar Disorder," March 25, 2009. www.clinicaltrials.gov /ct2/show/NCT00338806?term=bipolar+disorder+OR+man ic+depressive+illness+OR+bipolar+depression+OR+mood +disorders+OR+cyclothymic+disorder+OR+mania+OR +mixed+bipolar+disorder&recr=Open&fund=0&rank=4.

51. Anne Harding. "Ketamine Lifts Mood Quickly in Bipolar Disorder." Reuters Health, August 3, 2010. www.reuters .com/article/2010/08/03/us-ketamine-bipolar-idUSTRE67 25J820100803.

52. National Institutes of Health Clinical Center. "Double-Blind Placebo-Controlled Trial of Riluzole in Pediatric Bipolar Disorder," December 24, 2011. www.clinicaltrials .gov/ct2/show/NCT00805493?term=bipolar+disorder+OR +manic+depressive+illness+OR+bipolar+depression+OR +mood+disorders+OR+cyclothymic+disorder+OR+mania +OR+mixed+bipolar+disorder&recr=Open&fund=0&rank=1.

53. Depression and Bipolar Support Alliance. "Treatment Technologies for Mood Disorders," 2009. www.dbsalliance .org/pdfs/EmrgTechsBro09.FINAL.pdf.

Glossary

acute: A disease phase characterized by flare-up of symptoms.

anticonvulsive: A drug usually used to treat epileptic seizures but also effective in treating bipolar disorder.

antipsychotic: A drug used to treat psychosis.

chronic: A disease phase that is ongoing and long lasting.

cyclothymic disorder, or cyclothymia: A mild form of bipolar disorder.

depression: A state of extreme sadness and hopelessness.

electroconvulsive therapy: Medical treatment involving an electric shock to the brain that generates a seizure; the effect is a sort of "rebooting" of the brain.

gene: The part of a DNA molecule that passes hereditary information from parents to their offspring.

hypomania: A state of high energy and activity levels that are less intense than those seen in mania.

mania: A state of extremely high energy, optimism, and activity.

mixed state: A bipolar episode in which both mania and depression are present

neuron: A nerve cell.

neurotransmitter: A brain chemical that allows neurons to communicate.

psychosis: Mental disease characterized by an inability to distinguish fantasy from reality.

psychotherapy: Treatment of mental illness usually employing talk and behavior modification therapy.

rapid cycling: A condition where a bipolar patient has four or more episodes during a twelve-month period.

relapse: A recurrence of symptoms.

stigma: A mark of shame or discredit.

synapse: A tiny gap between nerve cells.

Organizations to Contact

American Academy of Child and Adolescent Psychiatry (AACAP)

3615 Wisconsin Ave. NW
Washington, DC 20016-3007
Phone: (202) 966-7300
Website: http://aacap.org

AACAP is an organization for mental health professionals; it also provides public information about mental disorders such as bipolar disorder that affect children and adolescents.

American Psychiatric Association

1000 Wilson Blvd., Ste. 1825
Arlington, VA 22209
Phone: toll-free (888) 357-7924
Website: www.psych.org

The American Psychiatric Association is a professional organization that represents psychiatrists, who are medical doctors who specialize in mental disorders. It also provides public information on mental diseases, including bipolar disorder.

American Psychological Association

750 First St. NE
Washington, DC 20002-4242
Phone: (202) 336-5500; toll-free (800) 374-2721
Website: www.apa.org

The American Psychological Association is a professional organization that represents psychologists, who hold a PhD in clinical psychology and are licensed to provide psychotherapy. The APA also provides public information on all aspects of mental health topics, including bipolar disorder.

Depression and Bipolar Support Alliance (DBSA)

730 N. Franklin St., Ste. 501
Chicago, IL 60654-7225
Phone: toll-free (800) 826-3632
Website: www.dbsalliance.org

DBSA is a nonprofit organization that seeks to better the lives of people with depression and bipolar disorder through support, education, research, and advocacy. Its website offers information on every aspect of bipolar disorder.

National Alliance on Mental Illness (NAMI)

3803 N. Fairfax Dr., Ste. 100
Arlington, VA 22203
Phone: (703) 524-7600; toll-free (800) 950-6264
Website: www.nami.org

NAMI is a mental health advocacy organization that provides support and education on mental illness for patients, families, and the public. It also promotes research and public policies that benefit people with mental illnesses. Its website has a wealth of information about bipolar disorder.

National Institute of Mental Health (NIMH)

Science Writing, Press, and Dissemination Branch
6001 Executive Blvd., Rm. 8184, MSC 9663
Bethesda, MD 20892-9663
Phone: (301) 443-4513; toll-free (866) 615-6464
Website: www.nimh.nih.gov

The NIMH is the branch of the U.S. government's National Institutes of Health that sponsors and conducts research on mental health and provides extensive public information on all aspects of mental diseases.

For More Information

Books

Patrick E. Jamieson and Moira A. Rynn. *Mind Race: A First-hand Account of One Teenager's Experience with Bipolar Disorder.* New York: Oxford University Press, 2006. Written for teens by a young man who was diagnosed with bipolar disorder at age fifteen; provides information about all aspects of the disease, especially about living with it.

Stefan Kiesbye, ed. *Bipolar Disorder.* Social Issues Firsthand. Detroit: Greenhaven, 2010. This anthology is aimed at teens and includes essays written by people affected by bipolar disorder.

Abigail Meisel. *Investigating Depression and Bipolar Disorder: Real Facts for Real Lives.* Investigating Diseases. Berkeley Heights, NJ: Enslow, 2010. This text covers all aspects of bipolar disorder, including personal profiles of affected people; written for teens.

Hilary Smith. *Welcome to the Jungle: Everything You Ever Wanted to Know About Bipolar but Were Too Freaked Out to Ask.* San Francisco: Red Wheel/Weiser, 2010. This book provides a sympathetic perspective on bipolar disorder; written for teens and young adults by a young woman with the disease.

Internet Sources

Kaity B. "Holding My Breath." Depression and Bipolar Support Alliance, June 2, 2011. www.dbsalliance.org/site/News2?page=NewsArticle&id=9095&news_iv_ctrl=1042.

Richard A. Friedman. "When Bipolar Masquerades as a Happy Face." *New York Times.* www.nytimes.com/ref/health/health guide/bipolar_ess.html.

National Institute of Mental Health. "Bipolar Disorder in Children and Teens (Easy to Read)." www.nimh.nih.gov/health/publications/bipolar-disorder-in-children-and-teens-brochure.pdf.

National Institutes of Health. "Major Ups and Downs." *News in Health*, May 2010. http://newsinhealth.nih.gov/issue/May2010/Feature1.

Stephanie Stephens. "Made for High Drama." *bphope.com* (blog). www.bphope.com/Item.sspx?id=559.

Nancy Tobin. "The Wit and Wisdom of Carrie Fisher." *bphope.com* (blog). www.bphope.com/Item.aspx?id=630.

Websites

Child and Adolescent Bipolar Foundation (www.bpkids.org/flipswitch). This website offers information and support for teens dealing with bipolar disorder.

Teens Health from Nemours (http://kidshealth.org/teen/your_mind/mental_health/bipolar.html). "Bipolar Disorder." The nonprofit Nemours Foundation website provides information on all aspects of bipolar disorder for teens.

Index

Picture Credits

About the Author

Melissa Abramovitz has been writing books and magazine articles for over twenty-five years. She is the author of more than thirty nonfiction books for children and teens, three children's picture books, and hundreds of magazine articles for all age groups.